THE HUNTER AND THE BRINGER

Morgan Straughan Comnick

Dedicated to: My friends who have never given up on me, encouraged my writing, and showed me light and talent I had when I still fail to see it. To those who laugh with me, comfort me, help me grow, and let me share all this love I have in my heart: Marissa, Kristen, Micah, Miles, Kate, Tabby, Nathan B., Andrew, Julie, Alesha, Cat, and Dan W.

I am blessed to have several people who care about me in my life and I can't wait to thank everyone in a dedication with more books to come!

CHAPTER 1

I love the feel of metal after it's sliced through the blood of the wicked on chilly nights.

Ribbons of rotting flesh danced down to the surface of the cliff, polluting the land with loud booms, the foul odor of decaying meat bringing down the thrill of my kill. Feathers spun dizzily before descending to the ground, the plumes confused on why they were free to wander the welcoming skies instead of being attached to a squawking master. I stepped over the chunks of inedible flesh and skin, avoiding the brushes of feathers with scary ease. I refused to let any of these disgusting reminders of this horrid being get near my body.

This *monstrum*.

I glared back at my kill, stabbing my distaste and loathing with my harden gaze, this filthy creature made out of the flesh of recently departed humans. I was grateful that this beast had its eyes closed when he crashed from the heavens by my might to its death. I could not bear to see the lifeless eyes that belonged to passed innocents who should be slumbering eternally in peace in their graves. I walked forward, away from the battle scene, this adventure closed on a happier note for mankind.

"Excellent job on this extermination as usual, Ms. Hemmingway."

Kesler hopped up towards me once I was off the cliff's edge and closer to the natural rock road. His light-brown hair and big eyes beamed with adoration, but his hands that held his memo pad and pen to record the incident shook like Arctic water was injected into his blood vessels. The poor kid was a brilliant data analyst and recorder, but he frightened so easily that it concerned me to have him out in the field.

I patted his shoulder with tenderness, a swelling of motherly affection warming in my stomach. For a boy three years younger than I, he liked to do things old school, something I admired. My hand went to adjust his brown corduroy vest on autopilot, smoothing out the wrinkles and fixing a loose button. "Thank you Kesler. It meant a lot to have such an observant recorder with me on this out of the blue attack."

As I finished my motions of pampering my colleague, a shadow popped up at an angle in front of me. My mouth smirked in secret for I knew the deep, raspy voice that would emerge from it. "It looks like your sword got a fair amount of blood on it, Ms. Hemmingway. Your form must have been off by a few degrees."

I lifted my head up to face our weapons specialist and combat trainer, Galen, his slick jet black hair in a ponytail and his golden eyes blinking once in the night, a falcon honing in on its prey. His look made the long scar from eye to chin come to life, its story haunting, yet, wanting to remain a mystery to the outside world. I kept my expression passive for his sake, his remark showing his brutally picky and perfect nature.

"Well, then you won't mind giving it a proper cleaning, eh *sensei*?" I held it out at arm's length with a thrust that made his hands twitch. At the last second, I grabbed my *katana* with ease and cocked my head mischievously. The fact I made this tough guy flinch was more beautiful than the glowing pink cherry blossoms that flowered on my handle. "Just make sure you give my *sakuras* some extra love. I don't want those lovely petals dull, now."

He grabbed the sword with a forced grunt, inspecting every centimeter of its ancient glory before gallivanting away to his portable workshop that was in the back of the van. Color drained from Kesler's face as he jerked his head back and forth between the widening space Galen had made between us. I ruffled his hair, the movement reminding me of leaves in fall swaying in the gentle breeze.

"Master Galen scares me. It amazes me how you can tease him at all!" His voice croaked in the middle, a frog nervous to jump off the safety of his lilypad.

"Psst! Yeah, I fight *monstrums* with the vile attempt to destroy mankind for a living. I think I can handle a grumpy weapons expert!" My hands landed on my hips, my breath blowing away a piece of loose hair that had got free from my silver moon hair clip in the fight. As if my motion beckoned them to appear, the chief's fancy car rolled up. The black paint gleamed in the moonlight, a spotlight showing that the boss had arrived in her usual late and does-not-give-a-damn style.

A gust of wind graced my face, cooling it with a tingling 'thank you' that I had purified the night air, the creature terrorizing this area now erased from this world. The tip of my blade, or any weapon we use in general, is dipped in a poison that is crafted in our laboratory. It not only slowly leaks into any *monstrums'* system every time I cut their flesh, feathers, fins, whatever they are deciding to wear, but after they are dead, the toxin in their bodies ignites and burns their remains from the inside. This allots us a few moments to record data and collect samples for the laboratory (that is also part of Kesler's job).

All that was left now was dustings of plucked feathers and some stains of blood that would soon melt into the rocks, discoloring them to what normal humans would assume to be from weathering. My eye caught sight of a large grey-white feather edged into a crack in the cliff. Attached to it was a chunk of meat the half the size of my palm. I needed to get rid of it. Something like that could raise suspicion. It was almost one in the morning and in a few hours, the early morning joggers would appear. Yeah, those running folks always seem to be the ones to find signs of the supernatural in horror movies. No reason to risk it.

Kesler always gives me a four ounce bottle of poison in case we have pieces of the *monstrum* that spread outside the main perimeter. I dropped three drops of the deep plum-hued liquid onto the feather and sealed the lid with caution as I watched the feather twist and bind into itself, as if in its own silent agony, the final frame of the live-action suspense film rolling its credits. Satisfied with my job, I stood up and brushed the dirt and gravel flakes from my hands, the last ember engulfing its fuel with a dazzling blaze.

"There! It looks like another job well done. Just have to put my stuff up in the lab at headquarters and then make sure Kesler has all the accounts right in his notes for the file. You rock Valda!" I cackled lightly at my punny remark, my hands on my hips once more as thoughts of a relaxing bubble bath and an episode of my latest anime filled my mind with joy and heart with glee . . .

"As lazy as ever I see, my little robin."

And the sweet visions I had just had erupted into raging hurricane waves and gory samurai death scenes when *his* vile voice entered my ears. I spun around, my teeth biting my bottom lip so I could have some physical pain to hold me back from smacking this asshole into next Tuesday, classic *Teenage Mutant Ninja Turtle* style (and I could use Michelangelo's techniques if I had my nunchucks with me).

There, in front of me, in all his annoying glory, was a man that I wish I had the legal right to knock down like the *monstrum* I slay: Jeremey Darington.

I refused to acknowledge his comment, afraid my voice would crack with anger and break the windows of the organization vehicles around us. I stared every inch of him down, from his stupid polished dress shoes, his crisp, modern black suit pants and light blue dress shirt, rolled up to his elbows like all those supermodels. His Ray-Ban sunglasses were attached to his collar like neckwear, winking in the headlights of the two white vans that I had just noticed pulled up next to my company's (I know, go me). His seaglass-toned eyes crinkled in amusement although his lips showered me with heated smugness in the form of a sweet, but devilish smile. The wind combed through his brown and gold spikes that should not work for a man his age, but the color was meshed so well that it was like they were just joined in holy matrimony.

He seemed delighted in my visual assessment of him, giving me a nod. Then, he added playfulness to his smirk as he tried to, discreetly, but wanting to get caught, run his eyes down my body. My purple flared long sleeved peasant top and beige knee-length skirt with light brown leggings most likely had rips and were covered in *monstrum* grime that I bet looked oh so mouth-watering. I willed myself not to blush at this jerk wad, my lips numbing from how hard I was chomping down on them. They would need some extreme T.L.C. from Dr. Yellow Cake Batter chapstick stat, once this loser was gone from my sight.

"Why . . . why do you always call me that?" Sure Valda, that is the best question to ask a total creep that you aren't supposed to ever interact with when he has brought a platoon with him. A+.

He flicked a tip of a thick spike of his hair with a flare that made me feel lower than dirt. "Because you will never be Batman, my dear."

Must. Resist. The. Urge. To. Pounce.

The sound of my boss's five-inch heels on the rocky pathway snapped me out of my primal bloodlust like a master leashing her dog. I sighed, the adrenaline rushing out of my body. My mind became clearer, seeing this saving grace as an opportunity to actually prove that I am productive, a pillar that helps my company stand, "What are you doing here, Darington?"

He took his Ray-Bans off of his shirt collar and began to absentmindedly hinging and unhinging the temples of them like putty in his hand. "Same as you. Here about the *monstrum* attack."

I grumbled, my hands clutching into fists. "You know that this isn't your company's area of skill and, as you can see like the overly pointy nose on your face, the *monstrum* isn't here. Once again, I do the dirty work and you guys want to take all the credit. Ain't gonna happen, slime bucket! Now, why don't you get the hell—"

"That's enough, Valda."

I stumbled at hearing my legal first name, my shoulders embarrassingly hunched over on command from the instructions of my boss. Chief Beryl Edric, the powerful woman in charge of our whole secret government unit, emerged next to us like a phantom in the night, in her usual fresh and standard black blazer, perfectly ironed white shirt, and black pencil skirt. Her slanted eyes branded into mine under her jet colored glasses. Her high, slicked back ponytail was so flawless, not a hair out of place as it swung to the motion of her calm breathing. She was beautiful and as scary as all get out, but she ran an organization that murdered vicious *monstrums* for a living and her mother, like her mother before her, was the councilwoman for her Native American tribe. Her family oozes with successful women.

She fit her job description very well.

Darington swiveled to meet me in front of the chief, a goofy, fake charming grin crawling up his face. He bowed to her, our queen of intimidation. "It is glorious to see you, Lady Edric." The sparkle in his eyes when he lifted his torso looked like it came right out of a manga. Gag me!

Like the kick-ass leader she is, Chief's face remained unchanged at his antics, but her eyes became smaller, darts aimed to stab his heart like the concealed knife she had attached to her hip. She could have whipped that out and wiped the floor with Darington, this fact dawning on him when he saw the slight lethal glimmer behind her glasses. He gulped, looking like a complete chump, and backed away to his original spot by me. It took all the strength I could muster not to grin like a monkey who won the last banana.

Chief turned her attention back to me, "Valda, Mr. Darington and his team are here for the same purposes we are, to investigate the *monstrum* attack and seek a way to stop it . . ."

She paused, this a signal to me to mean that they meddled, *again*. This *monstrum* was violent, had stolen four dead bodies that were just buried, preparing to enter their new afterlife. And it still craved for more, hunger consuming it, blinding it with greed, all these traits causing it to attack a neighborhood across the cliffside. I felt badly for Amy Bruckman, an incredible *kotodama*, a psychic with the power to control things with words alone. She was our group's kind-hearted guidance counselor that helped families who had their worlds flipped upside down with *monstrum* attacks or she helped us not be driven to insanity. Unfortunately, that was a real possibility and those who tried to leave with government secrets . . .

However, the way I noticed Chief's lip curve into a sneer ever so gradually meant that this was not the usual case and that she was not happy, but most surprising to me: she wasn't all powerful today. The fact that Beryl Edric could be powerless shattered my reality, like when a child learns Santa is a myth.

Seeing the turd monkey in a suit made my guts rumble with irritation, but Chief went over to him, striding over with her arms crossed. She did this during work often and looked like she was going to take over the world in this pose. As they began a discussion over what members of his organization were here, images of the tale I have embedded in my veins flashed in my mind, rolling like a film . . .

Our world coexists with monsters, or as my organization calls them since we like to stick with Latin roots, *monstrums*. As much as movies and books want you to believe the *monstrums* can become good, are peaceful, and may even fall in love with humans, it doesn't happen. They are creatures, like us, and they must survive, and they will any way they have to. I suppose, in that retrospect, they are not so different from us. But, every single *monstrum*, even ones that are calm in nature, such as fairies, guardian spirits, and such, were manifested, birthed from darkness. Humans, as strange as this sounds, were created from light. Our paths have intertwined so much since the original days of the planet that of course we would adopt and accept darkness into our world, but it is foreign. Every act of evil and tragedy, unless performed by nature or human hands or inventions, are caused by darkness and the *monstrum* and their minions.

7

I am not sure how our forefathers from the time of America's rise as a nation did it, but George Washington sent ambassadors out into the land to find the creatures he witnessed slaughter more of his men than the actual Red Coats (Louis and Clark are the most famous of these original monster documenters/hunters). They recorded data, drew illustrations, and were able to make compromises with the calm *monstrums* and the ones with intelligent thoughts, although those species can be tricksters. It was a challenge, but a very rewarding endeavor. Over time, with advances in science and technology, we were able to discover ways to find techniques to stop the *monstrums* that were still refusing to stay in the designated areas that the agreements stated.

With the world expanding with transportation, spatially the United States discovered that the other countries of the world have done similar contracts with *monstrums*. But, there were encyclopedias worth of new creatures, manifestations of malice, that were unique to each land. Asian units shared their information that they had found with us; that the creature had to *be* killed from a weapon that symbolized their culture. Such as a Japanese beast, it had to be a *katana*. Cave creatures? Clubs made of hard rocks and stones. The United Kingdom? Bows and arrows. And ours are guns. All weapons could damage raging *monstrums*, but using these weapons that corresponded with their origin made it easier. And when poison was tested and worked? It was a miracle for our cause.

The countries then decided to become a collaboration in 1893 and a secret government faction knew of the incidents. However, like with all things that came with politics, division occurred. World War II caused more than a war on soil, in sea, and sky, but it broke out too between those apart of the organization. The *monstrum* took the feuding as the perfect opportunity to feast upon the dead the travesty of this horrid war had caused, creating mass panic and the world needed much less of that. So, once the war was over in 1945, a split was decided upon by the government. Well, the small percentage who knows and monitors us. I'm honestly not sure that even our president is aware.

I belong to the group known as the *Sicarius Venator*, or in Latin, *The Assassin Hunters*. Our mission is to exterminate all *monstrums* that leave their designated homes, no ifs, buts, or coconuts. There has never been a time when it led to anything remotely good nor, unless they got to the scene quickly, there was never an encounter that did not have some bloodshed. The Hunters' labs spent time making stronger poisons for the *monstrum*, tougher weapons, and tracking down nests and packs in areas. Their employees train hardcore in all forms of martial arts and defense and all formats of weapons, from antiques to the latest. These creatures are made of pure darkness and they need to be destroyed at all costs. We are meant to protect mankind and allow the masses to live normal, arrogant lives.

Jeremey (Blah! His name sounds like acid in my tongue, even in my head) is a part of the other group, the *Justitia Lator*, or *The Justice Bringers*. Yeah, the name's not as badass as ours. Back on track, The Bringers refuse to kill the *monstrum*; they capture them and drag them away to their secret lab, seeing them as living creatures. They study them, interact with them, and their goal? To attempt to turn them *good*, like a B rated Disney movie (and I *adore* my Disney movies). They believe that *monstrums* can be tamed, can work alongside humans like they are some Pocket Monster. However, all their attempts have failed and they have lost loyal scientists, millions of dollars, and their labs have had more remodels than an O.C.D. interior designer. They have pulled the wrong lever in their methods of dealing with *monstrums* way too many times. Yet, they did collect bundles of data on our threats.

What a crazy, twisted universe I was thrown into, but it's not like I had a choice . . .

A snap echoed across my eardrum, making me leap out of my skin or similar to my darling cat if she got sprayed with water. On my side was stupid faced Darington. He bent down, his aftershave of sandalwood oddly intoxicating and way too close. I guess I stared for a few seconds longer to be socially acceptable because he gifted me with an endearing, cocky grin, one that stroked his pride that he was, in his mind, a stud. Good grief, Charlie Brown.

"Yoo-hoo! Big summer blow-out, princess! You need to pay attention, but I can understand if you want to rip my clothes off where I stand. Careful though, poppet...." He bent even closer to me, his breath chilled, like he just ate a breath mint. Whispering, making my skin prickly with a heat that felt feverish, he exclaimed, "The shirt is silk..."

My body shook with rage. "Dick!" and I spat on his oh so fancy shirt, stomping away towards my savior, Chief, who was signaling me over to her. Serves him right. The sound effect that popped out of his mouth that echoed in the night was so satisfying that I allowed the moon to see my secret smirk of tantalizing delight.

When I approached Chief, the slight souring pucker and millimeter lift of her brow told me that she was asking if I was okay. I responded with a baby-sized huff and shake of my head. Upon closer inspection, I saw that she was giving final directions to a member of The Bringer's crew, his crisp white shirt too blinding and unfit for our *monstrum* position. Seriously?! Have they never had to get out blood, guts, and feathers out of their pathetic, non-confrontational Scouts club? Gah!

The squeaky clean lackey bolted off to his company's soccer mom like van. Before I could inquire about this exchange, Chief spun on her heels and with no expression on her face, she voiced, "Status report?"

It took me a few more moments longer than I wanted to admit to blink off the dumbness that fogged my mind. After this relapse in common sense, I realized she was addressing the *monstrum* I destroyed before doltish Darington threw me off my track. Wish I could throw him off the cliff. I could totally cover it up.

"Oh. Yes ma'am." I stood taller, in our about face position, saluting her for the first fifteen seconds like protocol. "The *monstrum* was first reported to headquarters at 9:09 p.m., standard time. We arrived at the scene of last appearance by 9:37 p.m., which was one point three miles away from our current location. The *monstrum* had broken the windows of the four log cabins here that are rented out to campers and vacationers on the cliff-side, this area known for its nature hiking and views. Fortunately, only one family was here at the moment and we pulled up as the *monstrum* broke into their quarters. They sprinted out the back door and our side unit escorted them to safety down at our closest sister police station. The wind from the gusts the *monstrum* crafted was that of a winnow formation—"

The clomping of giant Armani dress shoes popped my perfect work bubble into microscopic pieces, embedding my shoulders with tension. I smelled the person behind the irritating noise before the voice horrified my ears, "What sort of monster was it?"

"An *onmoraki*, a bird demon from Japan. Its body is made of fresh corpses, this one consisting of four recently deceased souls that had not been buried yet." I answered automatically, giving him a scholarly glance, mildly stunned that I did respond to him so calmly. In addition, I was surprised he could not have figured that out from the fact I used a *katana*.

"Kesler has finished recording the details of his observations on the report and has the sample you provided chilling in our coolers for transport." Chief spoke, informing me that my end of the debriefing was complete. I set my hand up to my forehead in a final salute and gave her my full attention. Jerk Wad must have done the same behind me for I heard his oh-so-fancy shirt ruffle with movement. "It is time for departure so we can file this incident. Agent Hemmingway, you will ride in the main vehicle with Kesler and Galen. You know your arrangements Mr. Darington. Come along you two."

"Okay Chi . . . Wait . . . Hold up!" I took around five massive steps to get away from the now nauseating smell of sandalwood that was punching the inside of my nostrils. My foggy brain was not comprehending the reason for the words Chief spoke and why it sunk into my core and settled there. Something was awry in her final sentence, it a foreign bacteria that my cells needed to push out. "Two? Two of what?"

The way Chief spun and stared me at me point blank made a cold sweat mutate on my arms. I knew I better shut up unless I wanted my tongue wrapped around my neck. "Mr. Darington and his group will be following us back to our headquarters tonight. We have matters that need to be discussed at a secure location. Now, no more foolishness. I hate those who waste my time."

Then Chief was gone, breezing down to her glossy pitch-toned, half-a-million dollar sports car, owning the world like a model on a New York fashion week runway: intimidating, beautiful, and too powerful for someone of her short stature. I wish I knew how to bottle her spunk and sell it.

"Well, apple of my eye and the dot of my lower-case i, I suppose our force is too strong to pull apart. Let's get ready for an adventure, lollipop." And he skips past me, an idiot in the night, his whistling tunes coming forth from his annoying mouth pounding in my noggin slowly down to my eye sockets. The sigh that came out of me on its own made me feel like I had gained a hundred years in age. Dragging myself to the main Hunters van, with doe-eyed Kesler at my side and grumpy *sensei* taking the wheel and most likely endangering my life unbeknownst to me with his lead foot, I knew I was not looking forward to this 'adventure.'

Chapter 2

Twenty-eight minutes. That's how long it takes for Galen to pull into our headquarters in the middle of the country. It was a nice building that looks like it was made of black bricks. The paved rock driveway gave it a feel of mystery on top of its gothic class. The street lamps were Victorian and at night, when the moon shone and hit their tips, the shadows would cast shapes of classic *monstrums* on the dot times, such as 3:00 p.m., giving the world a secret peek into our true nature for sixty seconds.

Galen punched in the passcode on our garage opener in the van and went down to the basement floor once it activated. My mind zoomed like the images of the catacombs meant to confuse trespassers, a maze I knew as well as the poses of every Sailor Scout from *Sailor Moon*. It took all my willpower to not rest my head against the cool glass of our tinted window, wanting to feel the comfort to calm my fried nerves. I longed to grab my precious *katana* and stroke its metal, feel the centuries of battle it wore with the grace and beauty of a goddess, but I knew *Sensei* the Articulate would somehow put me in a one-handed headlock and still drive. I sadly have been on the wrong end of this oddity.

The van halted its advances and Galen cut-off the engine, the lack of hum from the motor making me feel empty. My time was really up. "We're here, kids. Get out of my weapon mobile and hurry up on the business. I want to go home."

Kesler and I hopped out of the van, poor Kesler clinging to his notebook until his hands were white, squeaking out a "Yes, sir," so quiet that I wouldn't have heard it unless I was walking right beside him. I gave Sir Buzz Kill a half-hearted wave as he went down the left side hall to his weapon's shop and vault. "Yeah, yeah, grandpa. We know it's past your bedtime. Stop being jelly of us and go polish your weapons until they are all pretty, pretty, shiny, shiny."

The way *sensei's* face crinkled into such a tall scowl even made his piercing scar wrinkle. Admittedly, it reminded me of a bulldog. It was utterly and weirdly adorable! I bit my tongue to not chuckle as he stuck his pointed nose in the air, grumbling, "Punk . . . Come by tomorrow morning, 4:30 a.m., for some extra drills." And he walked into his violent sanctuary, edgy and dramatic for a bulldog.

I shrugged and wrapped my arm around Kesler, escorting him to the hallway that led to our main base of operations. We scanned our ID cards, did fingerprints, and punched in our key codes, all while Kesler was mumbling and pleading with me about how I should not have made Galen mad. He wanted to take the blame for my extra sunrise training practice now. I brushed it off each time and patted his forehead playfully once, forcing a beam to show my co-workers busy at work that I could handle whatever Chief had in store for me. I got this. I plaster this smile on my face, I act respectful and approachable to tackle the world and this mess to the ground while still being a ray of sunshine. A deadly ray of sunshine, but still.

Kesler and I went to his cubicle, me sitting on the edge of his desk as I munched the string cheese I kept in his mini fridge in the corner. He began typing up his notes on his restored typewriter that had some modern bells and whistles to make it techy. Seriously, how precious was this kid? He was asking me for clarification once in a blue moon as I read over his shoulders, enjoying the tingling of the mozzarella cheese tickling my tongue with happiness. No wonder cheese is so drug worthy that science claims it is as addicting as morphine. I suppose I need to come clean; Hello. My name is Valda Hemmingway and I am a cheeseaholic.

I took a swig of the Yoo-hoo before I began towards this death sentence that would come with The Bringers. I ventured up the hall, glancing up and down for Chief in her usual monitoring stations that reminded me of a buffed up version of the NASA's mission control, what with its HD screens and DNA samples on wall scanners. It even had floating test tubes that encompassed the back wall of the room like a very unique wallpaper. Alas, before I got to Chief, who was gazing at the largest middle screen with a thoughtful and semi-perplexed look on her tanned face, a force pulled me back a foot and almost made me crash on my butt. However, I landed on something warm, solid, and slightly hard, or maybe *toned* would be a better description.

I shouldn't have turned around to answer my curiosity; it never does anything good for my cat or me. Leeched to my arm was the tapeworm of my existence: damned Jeremey Darington. Son of a monkey fiddle! Why can't he just explode already? He uses so much hair gel and spray. I bet I could get my lighter to spark a little self-defense fire and . . .

"Nice gigs, tartlet." His smile was that fake charming kind that made unintelligent girls swoon and made me about vomit in my mouth. I shook him off with ease and made my elbow a rapid point towards his eye socket, ready to give him a shiner, stopping myself before it made contact to show him I had control. He just stood there, his vision then peering into my irises with such a fun-loving amusement that I let out a grunt and Godzilla-stomped down to the main room with Chief, Captain Duck Spikes hot on my tail. I passed the other two members of his group, who gave me unsure nods of acknowledgement.

"Brother Ethan! Brother Seth! Bros!" I heard these boyish explanations roar behind me, the randomness of it making me screech on my breaks to listen for a heartbeat. An array of 'dudes,' 'man,' and 'what's up?' entered my ears and I wished desperately I could clean them out. The Bringers call us uncivilized because we get rid of foul creatures who are trying to murder us and now this? At least we use proper English and do not call everyone brother and sister like hippies. Freakin' bath salts.

"Friends! This is Val! Isn't she like the sexiest, most divine creature on the planet? Especially from the back . . . ? Yum-yum . . ."

I didn't know how it happened, but I somehow was being squeezed by Jeremey again. His fingers that were touching my blouse left a light burn of heat, a mark that made me feel branded, an imprint on my flesh that seemed too strange. I gulped, rapidly trying to locate the rational part of my brain that reacted in a nanosecond to danger and knocked it out cold to the ground. But, the circuits in my head were frantic, trying to decode the feeling of his hand on my shoulder. So, I picked the childish option.

I pinched his hand and twisted it behind him until he was on his tiptoes, the pain he was trying to hide slowly creeping into his face. This shift in power allowed me to take a cleansing breath. I released him hard, in front of his friends, his brothers, and walked away, my confidence spiking.

Until, the asshole opened his mouth flap again, "You know I get all the lovely ladies, but man! Val really takes the cake. Don't wait up . . ." and they hollered, or rather hooted and hollered, in The Hunters headquarters. Ethan and Seth praised this . . . this pig, about his talent to attract women. Jail may not look so bad right now if I could just beat the living hell out of him one time—

"Ah. Valda, Mr. Darington, I see you have come here together. I am glad you were able to locate each other." Chief gave a fraction of a smile, putting on her hostess face, but I knew from the way she squeezed her hands on her stomach and not under her chest that this whole collaboration was a whole bucket of horse hockey. It made her squeamish as well.

Hunters and Bringers . . . just don't go together.

"You wish to speak with us, Chief?" I kept my voice level to not have any of my distaste for the single cell organism saluting at least respectfully next to me show. Our science department had to pass by this main area here often, many going about their routine, but I could tell by their expressions that they were either stunned or enraged to see a Bringer here. Or, they pitied me. I'm not sure which was worse.

Chief turned towards our forced company, her eyebrow arched to act as if she was inquisitive about something. "What is your opinion on our facility, Mr. Darington?"

Dork-ington retreated a step backwards, a glued smile of uneasiness scratched on his cheeks. The way his lips and right eye slightly twitched, I saw the internal conflict that he was not sure to lie or to be blunt about his feelings of our establishment. I was not sure how I felt about that myself. "To be truthful, Madame Edric, it seems very . . . science-fiction to me, but the organization of your materials and security is something to marvel at."

Chief nodded, understanding his words. I looked up at him as well, a tad impressed with how he handled his statement. Not enough to acknowledge that verbally, but, hey; half a point to Slytherin for you, Bringer boy.

"I appreciate your sentiment, Mr. Darington. We pride ourselves here with our monitoring system in order to save as many lives as possible since *monstrum* attacks are sudden, never planned or informed to us in advance, as you know." Jeremey gave a solemn nod to this, agreeing with Chief. A wave of sadness rolled in his eyes, but only for a second, an invisible moon pulling it back. I never pondered on why Jeremey was in the *monstrum* business in the first place. We all have our reasons, stories, drives, but they are rarely voiced because most of us . . . don't have good things to share.

I blinked away my inner Shakespearean, borderline sappy monologue and readjusted my focus to the woman with the ice stare that signed my paychecks. Chief lowered her head, a *sensei* demeanor radiating from her that made her voice captivating to listen to, your body engrossed in the knowledge she was about to shower us with, "For as long as our history has been recorded, *monstrums* have been a primal, animalistic form of darkness that shares our world. We understand their desire to live, but they also tend to have a thirst for blood, striking when they like. A few races, most with intelligent thought and mannerisms similar to our own, do not show this bloodlust as often, but, they have the power to do so . . ."

"The most powerful demon is the one that looks human . . ." I spurted off absent-mindedly.

Chief gave me a shake of her head, showing approval. Sandalwood Man stared blankly at me, like I had grown a second head. Good! Maybe I can use it to peck his liver out. "Where in the world did you hear that expression?"

"When . . . when I was studying in Japan . . ." I mumbled, turning away from him so he couldn't see the rose-heat that was crawling up my face. I didn't want him to know it was a quote from one of my first animes, *InuYasha*. Although, I had read like statements in books my *sensei* in Nihon had in his beautiful library study with my time over in the Land of the Rising Sun.

"Along with this theory goes with it an additional list of concerns. With what we are aware of, *monstrum* attacks are from *monstrums* with average or beast-like thoughts, savage, not calculating or patient. Yet, we also know that *monstrums* such as fairies, guardian spirits, and others, have the abilities or some attributes that could make them deadly to our kind if they unleashed it. That is why we made contracts with them first after the Revolutionary War, a contract with the devil, so to speak, for them to leave us alone. With their help, they can translate for the majority of the *monstrums* we deal with as well."

I didn't understand where this was coming from. Chief watched activity around the clock and both organizations knew the movements of roaming and nomadic groups of primal and intelligent *monstrum* fairly quickly. "I don't understand Chief. Are you concerned about these intelligent *monstrum* that we have had contracts with for a few centuries deciding to use their powers, that they have been lurking for the right opportunity?"

"You are as right as you are lovely, Ms. Hemmingway, a flower blossoming in the moonlight."

A compliment like that would have had Jeremiah-The-Bullfrog down on the floor with his nose smashed, but it did not come from Darington. No, it was from the kindly grandfather figure that was wheeling his way steadily to us, Mr. Wren Stillman. Mr. Stillman was the equivalent of my Chief, the leader of The Bringers. For a group that left a foul taste in my mouth and a roll for my eyes, he was refreshing. He was in his late fifties, but still looked polished, the mannerisms and smile of a true gentleman, his lake-toned blue eyes always dancing with light and wisdom. He reminded me a lot of Mr. Rogers. Actually, he even wore the sweater vests that Mr. Rogers was so famous for! I had never heard him yell or get stern and nothing seemed to bring him down, even the fact he was forever in a wheelchair due to a *monstrum* attack. I secretly admired his spirit very much.

"Father Stillman." Jeremey approached and bowed at the waist with longing and respect deep inside his voice. His hand was made into the sign language sign for peace and he placed it proudly on his chest. He looked very noble in that moment and it made my breath catch, to see Dud Darington looking so loyal and knightly. At least he knew how to respect his boss, I suppose. Maybe another half point awarded to his House.

"Brother Jeremey, it is good to see you." Mr. Stillman took the monkey's forearm and shook it, his eyes ablaze with tenderness. "It is so good to see you here. And Ms. Hemmingway," He gave me a grandfather beam and patted my hand sweetly, reminding me of my papa. I graced him with a smile to match, his touch putting me a bit at ease. "It is always a dear pleasure for this old soul to see you. Your brains, brawns, and beauty are worthy of legend, but make sure you take care of yourself." I gave him a small, quick curtsy, knowing I can play it off with him. I am always perplexed with imagining him with any *monstrum* group in general, but I can tell his heart, in his mind, is in the right place.

He wheels a few paces closer and to the right to gaze upward at Chief, his eyes flickering with light that match the same intensity of the shimmer from her glasses. "Beryl, an honor to be amongst your fine staff. Thank you for the invitation to host this gathering and including myself and a few of my members as well."

Chief stared at him longer than what most would call normal, but her look was not one of harshness or strict business. Although her facial expressions did not change, her eyes grew softer, like rich, moist soil, her only response being a simple, "You are welcome."

My head ping-ponged between this short, but what felt like an eternity eye lock. I sensed something was sizzling invisibly from myself and Dorkulous between our two bosses, but that could've been a misdiagnosis on my part. Being the main two leaders of the two American *monstrum* groups, one would assume they had similar attributes and stresses to running it, a connection others would not comprehend.

Jeremey leaned forward, his eyes intense with sudden interest. "Father Stillman, you look as fetching as ever in your forest green sweater vest."

Urgh! Why is it every time this bozo opens his pie hole, I want to slam an actual pie down his throat?

Mr. Stillman didn't miss a beat, "Thank you. I got it at Kohl's"

"And I am sure it was a tremendous deal, but I would like to please be informed as to why we are having a meeting here and what it entails. Ms. Hemmingway, although as pretty as a picture, needs to change her clothes." Jeremey gave me a look of innocence, that his comment was all for my safety, but by the way he crinkled his nose and his eyes skipped like a trickster leaving town with a bag of gold, his honesty, for my sake intent was all a pony and stage show.

Unclear by his meaning, I glanced down to inspect my outfit. My purple flared long-sleeved peasant top and beige knee-length skirt with light brown leggings was spotted with splashes of internal organs, blood prickles, grime, and mud that looked like it was mixed with . . . mucus? You know what, I did *not* want to know. I had a small snag on the embroidery of my skirt, a rip the length of my thumb on my right shoulder, and my shoes were crusted with gunk. I suppose I should have inspected myself more closely in the pitch black van. At least I flattened my hair from its winded tangled ungodliness.

I just hope I didn't smell, like rotten eggs or vomit or even lemon pledge. Yuck!

"I mean, it doesn't really seem . . . combat ready, if you ask me." He voiced as he rocked on his heels, his eyes pretending to be interested in the ceiling like he was mapping out constellations.

I puffed up my cheeks like a Jigglypuff after she gives a concert and everyone rudely falls asleep. How dare he question my fashion sense and look closely enough to even make a comment? The nerve of this ape! "I was at a P.T.O. meeting and fundraiser for a new creative arts room in a school close to my town, helping to pass out cookies to our visitors when I got the call, thank you very much. It's none of your business about my clothing choices, anyway."

My lips puckered in a sour pose and I shifted my vision a centimeter to give him the cold shoulder without looking like a non-team player. I felt his body stiffen next to me, his annoying natural heat radiating away from me with my action. I did not realize I had adapted to his body heat being in close quarters with mine to begin with. Stupid Jeremey!

Chief stood up taller, looking massive now despite her small structure and frame. "To answer your question, *Mr. Darington*," she hissed out before she continued, "we have strong suspicions that local abductions in the area, although not close enough to be on the immediate target for police nor following a pattern of areas, people, gender, or social classes, are due to an intelligent *monstrum*."

"A *lamia*."

My heart leapt out of my chest and into my throat, beating, pulsing, every deadly beat of that final, mind blowing conclusion Chief voiced. I lurched forward, unable to control my body's movement any longer, the intensity of the situation weighing too much for my soul to bear.

"But how?" I blurted loudly.

"What does this mean?" Darington's voice blended with mine as he started his sentence half of a nanosecond after my own, our words meshing, colliding into a mixture of fear.

Chief sealed her eyes away from us, trying to blind the stress I could see throbbing in her forehead. She was getting a headache, something that rarely happens to her since she works out and uses her tribe's natural herbs and medicines to cure anything, but she dare not show weakness by rubbing her temples. A sigh was about to pass her lessening in tone ruby lips, but Mr. Stillman rolled an inch closer to us, all attention now on him in our inner circle.

"Every time any harm or tragedy affects mankind, we are there to monitor it, defend it, in our different ways, as guardians of the secret of monsters. Both groups want to protect our precious Earth and those living on it, so our systems and team of experts are to document and report anything out of the norm for a perfect society. It is not for certain if a monster is at fault, but the possibility, especially an intelligent one, is reason to further investigate.

"The only thing we know about the kidnapped victims is that they are all led to forested areas, areas that have miles of trees and then large clearings or caves that are hard to track, rarely on maps. Of course, we have had surveyors go inspect these claims and see if they find any of the missing persons, but alas, no such luck has arose. And there is a mist, a white cloud of mist that traces the outlines of their bodies and follows behind them like a cape or veil. Then, they vanish just as quickly as they come into view, phantoms in the night."

My gaze became steely, understanding Mr. Stillman's message in his administration-like speech. "*Lamia*, the term we use for vampire, although *lamia* technically is a female creature in most myths, have the ability to conquer mist to conceal themselves and their prey, but not entirely. However, they can do it from great distances and without much thought or energy, leading their victims to many locations of their choosing. It is like the people are under their control, their mind lost, to only follow the pulls of the *lamia's* hypnotic glare. It is . . . quite a power."

Chief regained her composure, giving Mr. Stillman's wheelchair a fast tap to inform him she would take over, making him sigh and go back to his overly gentle-hearted grandfather smile that made me want to sit down and have cookies with him. She lifted her glasses to the bridge of her nose, demanding our full attention at her dominance once again. "It is indeed scary to picture and it makes us wonder why they have never used this ability on such a massive scale before. They are eternal creatures, so waiting for a few centuries seems like months most likely to them, an insignificant amount of time, but we have no hardcore evidence to know if it is this *monstrum*, a *lamia*, or another variety. Regardless, we wanted this manner looked into since it is not high enough on police investigation to draw immediate concern for mass panic yet and the pieces of the puzzle do not fit, but they smell of *monstrum* activity—"

"And that is where you, our two best, come into play." Mr. Stillman continued, gifting Darington and I with a kind half-smile and affectionate voice, like he was giving us a great treasure.

"Mr. Stillman and I have been discussing that, for this one odd, critical case . . . having our organizations team up and we . . . we feel we can only trust our best agents for this job and . . . that is the two of you, Agent Hemmingway and Mr. Darington." Chief said it as cut and dry as hacking a brittle stump with a sharpened axe blade, but that didn't make the blow any less painful and sanity shattering.

"Wait . . . So Jerk. . . . I mean, Mr. Darington, and I would have to work together to see if we can track down any clues of *lamia* breaking their contract or whomever is responsible for these kidnappings and put a stop to them?" I was surprised my mouth was able to produce sound since my limbs were shaking and I felt like I had been zapped with a lightning bolt.

Chief refused to look me in the eye, her ponytail swaying, the muscles in her face tense, stretched out in stress. From the baby quiver in her lip, I could tell she felt like she betrayed me, and sadly, my heart was hammering its agreement. She spoke, despite the air being so thick, clogging our lungs, "That is a correct description, Agent Hemmingway." From the glare due to the glint in her glasses, Chief hushed my urge to rebut, snuffed it out like an ember that had no chance to thrive in a fire.

"Our legal and coverage departments will take care of how to get your new roles in place," Mr. Stillman explained in his elegant, calming manner that made me want to vomit and fall under its effective spell at the same time, a yin-yang clash of irritation and soothing emotions placed in my chest. "But, regardless, you will be close enough to do investigations and whatever the mission entails from your cover-up positions with your O.N.J.s"

The O.N.J. (Organization Number Job) is something both groups' field agents (other than administration) have. They are real, white or blue collar jobs that allow us to watch the general public for their own protection from unbeknownst to them *monstrum* by us blending in with those who had normal lives, lives we used to have, foreign to agents and members now. I am fortunate that I got stationed in a position that I have a degree and license in, a career I had dreamed of since I was in intermediate school.

"Don't worry Father Stillman, my new goddess and I will *partner* up, in every manner, no matter the strain." The ego in his tone and the way he thrusted his nose outward like a conceited superhero sent shooting pains down my intestines and a croaking sound come out of my throat. My Lord, he was so repulsive that he almost made me choke on my own spit. What a baboon-butt bastard!

Mr. Stillman shut his eyes lazily and gave our rectangle a solemn nod. "I am happy to hear you put the mission at such high importance despite the unheard of circumstances, Brother Darington. We are your direct contacts for this assignment, so any information you find, no matter how small, or any issues you come across, you know how to reach us on your licensed phones." His eyes shifted to gaze into mine. They were small, squinted, but were such a delightful crystal blue that it made me feel like I was a flower, dehydrated and desperate for the perfect sip of water to flow into my roots and his pools, Mr. Stillman's, was it.

"Ms. Hemmingway, The Bringers are grateful for your cooperation in this assignment. I will not go into a monologue on how important it is to protect mankind from monsters. Your sense of duty shines like a beam of moonlight on a sparkling lake, but please, do what your heart tells you."

"My agent follows her gut and instincts, which is why she is the top notch of my A listers. I have no doubt she will succeed in this mission." Mr. Stillman looked at Chief after she spoke. Chief was a woman of influence and power, a true pillar of integrity. Chief felt incapable of lying, but the dispirit expression his pupils were shimmering at my lady boss. I felt like they had stolen a key component to this mission, a piece of this puzzle that affected more than mankind, but myself, a sliver of my essence—

"Valda!" I snapped out of my thoughts, now in attention, blinking rapidly to find my composure. I hadn't realized my mind wandered to the point that I spaced out more than the aliens in *Space Jam*. She cleared her throat with annoyance and shame, her sound making a blush wedge into my cheeks from embarrassment. Chief placed her hands behind her back to continue, "Your O.N.J. will be the same, so you are free to go to get some rest for the remainder of the night. Mr. Darington, if you do not mind staying for a tad longer, we would like to discuss your new O.N.J. position for this assignment."

"Righty-O!" Said the thorn in my side with so much pep that he hopped in the air and his hand landed in a goofy salute, reminding me of a million times less adorable version of Sora from my beloved *Kingdom Hearts* games.

I did my salute to Chief and shook Mr. Stillman's hands professionally, but with a little smile I could not hide before zooming away. Jeremey's despicable voice rang through the open air space, his fake hooting making me wish I had my taser to stick in my ears, or in his cake hole, whichever was more convenient. I was done with all him and The Bringers bulls—

"Ms. Hemmingway!" Kesler's slightly trembling voice in front of me shook me out of my clouded state. I hadn't even realized I was two cubicles away from his. I must have been fuming so hard that he sensed my bad vibe. His little face was twisted in nervous wrinkles and flushed while his fingers jittered around his vest, as if he was buttoning the air around them.

My anger cooled about thirty degrees just seeing him. I pushed the tension headache that was pulsing to a compartment in my mind and went into big sister mode.

"Thanks for meeting up with me, Kesler. Good work on those documents. I know you aced the case!" I gave him a cheesy grin and tousled his soft hair once more, loving how it moved so effortlessly in my hand.

He whimpered a tad, but his eyes were brimming still with concern and a burning desire to ask more. "Is everything okay?" He choked out, his voice climbing up an octave.

I poked his nose with my index finger, making him blink rapidly, a puppy spazzing from content confusion, before walking past him to his office space to retrieve my hoodie and Hello Kitty work tote. "Everything will be peachy, Kesler. The assignment is a Level 8. Ace C, but The Bringers will be staying around for a while for this mission, at least, a few of them. I am sure Chief will inform everyone tomorrow after we all had some rest." I presented with a warm smile before grabbing some string cheese for the road and pecking his cheek. This made him go into a fury of blushes and stuttering. He was too darling! With him here, it made the hole in my chest from missing my parents and brother, Darius, who was only a year younger than Kesler, fill up a smidgen.

As I adjusted the weight on my shoulders, sore from tonight's outings, I calculated if it was truly worth it to even go back home. I had to be back here in about two and a half hours thanks to Mr. *Sensei*-the-Cracky-Prick and it takes me about a half hour to get home from headquarters, even with my speedy company ride, a Kawasaki Ninja ZX-11/ZZ-R1100 that can go up to 176 miles per hour.

However, I most likely needed to take a shower and get workout clothes. To confirm this, I took a gander at my now tattered rags, letting out a huff. What an annoyance! I've had this top and skirt for years and really liked them. Thank gosh we have an amazing laundry and clothing unit that could mend any material. On top of all this, I had to prep my bag, outfit, and lunch for my day job that I had to be at by 7:00 a.m. I let out another sigh, seeing I really did have to go home, but there was no way I was getting even a cat nap in. At least, if I venture home, I could avoid Stupid Face McStupid Nuts for a bit. I better *vámonos* before he finishes talking to Chief.

I kicked it into gear, shoving the events of tonight with the *monstrum*, The Bringers, and He-Who-Will-Not-Be-Named out of my brain. I smiled into the blinding lights at the end of our driveway and into the night lofty breeze, imagining the wonderful day I had planned at my day job, the perfect job for someone with my set of skills.

CHAPTER 3

"*There is no time for snoozing, there's work to do. Spring time has come to the Zippy Zoo!*" I sang, clapping to the joyous sounds of my students' giggles.

"Alrighty friends! It's time to go to our seats for writing time. Please get out your pencils and put that bubble in your mouth before I count to ten so we can get a cat sticker for our class Awesome Sauce Behavior Party Poster! We are so close to getting those 60 stickers! Hurry, my little bookworms! 10 . . ." and with that, they scattered like bugs, getting into their writing routine.

I walked slowly around my classroom as I counted, patrolling their sweet, frantic little antics all to get a sticker in the likeness of my real furry baby, Socks. I gave Chloe a finger to my lips through a knowing smile to tell her to shush as I counted to 3. She covered her mouth overdramatically, making me give her a wink as I moved on. Before I hit one by the white board and our Awesome Sauce Behavior Party Poster, I saw Liam struggling to get in his seat, him being so small. I patted his back and gave him the little momentum he needed to sit down without missing a beat.

"And . . . Zero! Excellent job friends! That's one more cat sticker on our poster. Give yourselves a quiet pinky party for a job well done." They silently wiggled in their seats, jamming to the music in their little noggins for five seconds. I clapped to get their attention back to me, continuing our lesson on how to properly write a Z in manuscript format, my hands and mouth on autopilot, a script I long knew by heart. My brain drifted to happy, bubbly thoughts of how these precious little ones warmed my heart and made everything worthwhile. I had to cling to that bubble to keep my eye from twitching. The stress of my night job caused this sometime.

I know what you're thinking: Umm, yeah, *hell* no. If I was a parent, there is no snowball's way I would let my sweet angel from Heaven above be taught by someone who has a third degree black belt in seven different martial arts as well as top notch training in other fighting and defense styles. Moreover, I am labeled as a firearms, blades, and assorted weapons usage mistress. Well, that's all fine and dandy, but I never decided when I was my students' age that I was going to kill *monstrums* for a living. I would have found another way to promote justice, like charity events or becoming a Power Ranger, Sailor Scout, and/or *Pokemon* Master (still working on fine-tuning that job description, but it's coming along rather swimmingly).

No, I have wanted to be a kindergarten teacher since I was ten, between my father being a teacher and my favorite teacher telling me I had the compassion to educate. After that, I knew it was the job for me. I always had young cousins and we would play school at my grandma's all the time. It was a blast, seeing their eyes light up and beaming smile when they learned something new. I love being creative and making my students enjoy school while instilling love and lifelong values in them. Plus, this is a great place to wear my cosplays and do my array of humorous voices during story time. *No one* judges at kindergarten. The lamer, the better!

I swiveled fully around after my writing Z explanation to absorb their little faces, them the sunshine my wilting soul needed. I went to college for four years to be a teacher, joining The Hunters after I graduated. This is my passion, education, and I was thrilled when after working as a special education paraprofessional at my local middle school for two years (a job I really cherished), my company helped me find this position since I had my certification. I got the job on my own merits and The Hunters allow it to be my O.N.J.

These children are the reason I do what I do for The Hunters; to save their future.

"And that is how we finish our lowercase z. Good job listening, my little bumblebees. Go ahead now and get out six different colored markers to trace your rainbow Z workpage. Please raise your hand high to the sky if you have a question, but Ms. Hemmingway will be calling a few friends to her desk to help them write their name. Let's make smart choices everyone. Zander, let's start with you, good sir."

I strode over to my purple wooden desk, its silver star and moon accents winking in the sun from my window. Zander shuffled up to my desk, eager to hand me his paper, but his dark brown eyes looked sad, like he was in trouble. I patted his shoulder so he would look at my face. "You have done such a beautiful job on your name this week. I am so impressed with how much you've improved! Now, let's get this lowercase *e* all pretty so your name can be an all-star!"

He stood by the extension tray attached to my desk, focusing hard on each pencil mark. Pointing out ways to guide him while watching my students work to start their journey through life, my tension and tiredness melted away for the moment. Sure, they would hit me like four monster trucks once I putted my way home after grading, but right now, the only thing that mattered at this second was encouraging Zander to practice his *e*.

* * *

"Howdy, Hemmingway Stars!" I heard this shout of introduction after I gave my line ender, Jack, a fistbump for helping our art teacher pick-up a paper she dropped before the door shut, my students inside their special class.

"It's Hemmingway-sensei *hoshis*." I mumbled by impulse, lucky no one was around to see the steam coming out of my nose and ears. *Hoshi* is Japanese for star, one of my obsessions. Hemmingway. *Hoshi*. Makes sense. But, alas, no one will refer to us as that. One day, my *chibi hoshis* will rule this school.

It was now my planning period after a busy restroom break and I was secretly debating if I wanted to crash and take a nap, but from Lindsey Coleman's bubbly demeanor, I knew she wanted to gossip about something. Her pretty, super thick and perfect golden beach waved hair swayed as she glided over to me in her cheery sundress, her clearwater eyes sparkling more than an in-love maiden against her porcelain skin. Lindsey was a good friend of mine, but looking down at her (her short size was the only physical part about her that didn't make me feel bad about myself), I felt like I belonged in a sewer to her white pearl castle overlooking the forest of beautiful, thin people and glittery unicorns.

"Having a good day, girlie? It's incredible how well-behaved your kiddos are." Her grin lit the hallway as we stepped to the side by the massive bay window, rooting our feet for casual banter.

"Epic so far, knock on wood. Your chickadees were showing such good manners waiting at the water fountain" Yeah, us kindergarten teachers have stimulating conversations.

She leaned in, her Chanel Coco Mademoiselle perfume tickling my nostrils. "Did you hear the big news? Principal Ohlinger is gone."

"Like, she's ill or left suddenly?" I arched my eyebrow for clarification. Mrs. Ohlinger had a nasty fall last year trying to hang something and she never has fully recovered from it. Now, her son that just started college is going through chemotherapy for liver cancer. None of us would blame her for needing a breather. The woman is a blessing to our little ducklings. She is so kind and colorful in her printed moo-moos, floral headbands, and long puka shell necklaces. Her oversized tortoise glasses and long, sandy kinky hair made her the warm, hippie face for our school, an excellent boss.

Still, her leaving without giving us a formal, well-composed, sentimental email with too many cute emojis three days ago made a bad feeling sink in my stomach.

"No, she's officially *retired*. Apparently, the board held an emergency meeting late last night after the fine arts fundraiser we were at and approved it."

"*Eh?*" I screeched out, clamping my mouth shut before I could start rant-shouting in Japanese. How is this even possible? I decided to state the obvious. "That's never happened before. I mean, I know she needs to take care of her son, but today is Wednesday. I figured she would inform us on a Friday and then be gone by Monday, to make our week even."

"Girl, I *know*!" Lindsey stressed, her eyes engulfing her heart-shaped face. "She's so punctual. But, none of that is the craziest part! They already hired our new principal to replace Mrs. Ohlinger!"

"What now?! How is that even possible?! It usually takes three weeks to hire a new person between the writing prompts, interviews, and hiring committee and school board decision. You can't pull principals from thin air!" I could feel the creases of shock appearing on my face.

"Girl, *I know*! And, get this. We have a *male* principal, at a kindergarten, and he's here, *today*! Apparently, tutoring has been canceled so we can all meet him officially at a staff meeting."

The fact our principal was a man didn't bother me; I am all for gender equality both ways. But, the fact that we not only get a new principal from nowhere, but the fact it's a man, for the youngest students in the district, was an oddity even in the unique store. There goes my cat nap idea; the speculations and chatter of ten female teachers will be the topic of our plan time now.

"I got a glimpse of him; he's pretty foxy." This came from Christy Rockington, my beloved school partner-in-crime, her blend of sweet and sassy rolled into one, perfect person.

"Umm, honey, I can use some beef cake in my life. Let's see what this fella brings." Coming into light behind Christy was Sherri Craft, my school mentor and adoptive school momma. I referred to her as Momma Bear because no one gets to her babies without facing her claws. She embraced me into her plump bosom, cradling me like a too tall child. I escaped her grip after a few seconds of warmth, getting my ducks in a row on our whirlwind situation.

"So, new, guy principal, out of the blue. Meeting him after school to just swear our allegiance to his kindergarten army. Got it." I gave a thumbs-up, blinking my eyes in a consenting fashion that was as fake as the meat in Dollar store frozen dinners.

Christy cupped her mouth to suppress the loud cackles she was known for, but she failed miserably, draping her slender arm over my shoulder so I was pulled downward, forced to be more level to her face. "And foxy! Don't forget that he's foxy."

"You sure like that word. Is that the word of the day for *Sesame Street*? I thought it was empathy and potato according to my curriculum schedule."

"Honey, I don't care if he's an ogre. If he does his job right and has testosterone, then this momma will be a happy camper. I'm over all the slobbering ape behavior I've had to deal with over this divorce." Sherri slid her glasses down seductively at no one in particular, arching her eyebrows alluringly down the hall, as if beckoning this newcomer to sail into our shores. I know her divorce has been hard on her, him being a cheating bastard who used his Scottish accent for evil, but I still didn't understand why the fact our principal was a man was getting her all excited in the panties. We don't even know how old this dude is!

On a side note, I do hope he's *not* an ogre. They smell like rotting goats, sour grapes, and dried glue. Plus, the fact they liked to roll in the dirt and kill things with their giant clubs like they were the main hitter for a *monstrum* baseball league, the Killer Sluggers, was disgusting. Yeah, not good company.

Lindsey hopped up, letting out a baby squeal that reminded me of a pageant piglet in a bonnet. "Ooooh! This will be such a change, but if we could have a Dr. McDreamy rule over us, then I'd be—" She stopped mid-sentence, her mouth hanging so low that I bet she was attracting more flies than men. With her eyes aglow and her delicate fingers a twitter, she tapped my shoulder with her fake Hollywood rose pink nails, "Oh my goodness! Speaking of ... Here he comes, from down the other end of the hall!"

All three of them crowded in front of me to get a closer look, but they left me a space if I wanted to glance. I really wasn't interested. I would meet the man soon enough and I dealt better with formal encounters where politeness dominated, not who could twirl their hair the best or show off their rack like a champ. In the four years since I have been with The Hunters, dating, relationships, and romance didn't tickle my fancy. I liked observing budding love bloom, either in the real world or in my animes and mangas, it placing me in a bubble of rainbow happiness.

I didn't need to be apart of a twosome. It wouldn't be the same with someone——

"Good night! He's a hunkasaurus!" Christy exclaimed through clenched teeth so only our gaggle of girls would hear. She fanned herself with her hand, her cheeks actually a pale pink hue.

"It looks like I will be going to that meeting early, ladies, to get the best seat in the house for all those angles. I gotta inspect them thoroughly." Momma Bear Sherri was almost rumbling with anticipation, making 'mmm' sounds every time she got a different view.

Lindsey just kept mumbling to herself on what to say, acting like a lovesick teen at her first major boy band concert and her idol was approaching her. It took all my mental strength to not roll my eyes. Is this how women act, fawning over men like they are a prize? I guess that's why I'm the fuddy-duddy, antisocial in the group. I just don't get it.

"Val, you have to check him out!" Lindsey clapped her hands together against her sparkly lips, I'm sure smearing her flawlessly applied gloss. I sighed internally, sick of her jabbing me with her bony elbow. I suppose I could at least look to know the face of my new boss ...

And then, the world stopped spinning and my organs froze over.

Strutting in front of us was the devil reincarnate if he used too much hair gel and had a lazy grin that made bar flirts look more appetizing: Jeremey Freakin' Darington.

I blinked so much that water stung my eyes, but I had to drown this nightmare out. I had to be trapped in a nightmare. I haven't slept in nearly forty hours and I had an intense workout for my punishment thanks to *sensei* being a hardass. Maybe I got hit in the head too many times when we did our boxing sparring and it's now just sinking in. Or, maybe I'm on drugs, someone slipping something into my string cheese. I did have two pieces with Kesler. Or, maybe I needed to get on drugs, something that gave me illusions of being a Disney Princess in Tokyo, riding Simba across Venus as we quote lines from *Hamlet*.

Yeah, illegal illusions sound better than my reality right now.

No matter what I did, there he was, twelve feet in front of our pack, walking achingly slow like a runway model and the world was his eternal catwalk to work his stuff. I made myself rigid in stance and mind, trying to blend into the background of my excited estrogen circle, calming myself into a laser, critical focus I used for *monstrum* nest observations.

I loathed how he owned the suit he was wearing, it pressed and polished to the point that Tim Gunn, my *Project Runway* idol, would tell him he made it work, much to my dismay. *Et tu,* Tim Gunn? The Michael Kors designer style was unmistakable, the jacket, pants, and vest fitting him to the T, the navy color bringing out the pop in his seaglass-green-toned eyes. However, other than his professional suit and Armani military shiny dress shoes, he had a mint green button down shirt under his vest and an orange sherbet necktie, spicing his outfit up with some fun that reflected our school. His hair was even spiker today, if that was even possible, the blond and brown once again harmonizing into a new color. Their shade reflected the sunlight through the bay window behind us as much as his silver and gold Gucci watch.

He looked polished and easy, a professional and a person who went with the flow. How he balanced both personalities in one look was beyond me.

Darington the Dolt stopped a foot short in front of Lindsey, eyeballing her with glee with his cocky twinkle in his eyes and a charming, cool smile on his lip. Lindsey looked like a piece of chocolate that was left out in 120 degree weather. She was going to be a puddle of goo in a few moments and I did not want to wipe her off my shoes.

"Good morning, ladies. It's a pleasure to bump into such a fine group of educators on my first day here." He threw his arms outward dramatically, as if overcome with emotion, praises he wanted to sing about us. El grosso. "I look forward to working with you as your principal at this fine school. Christy!" He placed his fingers under his chin cutely and gave her a Little Rascals wave. "It's great to see you again. And Sherri, your reputation does not measure to the grand presence that stands here before me."

Christy started a fit of flirty half giggles so spazzy that I thought she was having an asthma attack. Sherri merely nodded, with a smile all her own that showed she was going to dominate the universe, and Jerkules was going to be her slave boy. Another point for Momma Bear.

"My I ask your name, my lady?" Jeremey aimed his question at Lindsey, whose tiny body was about to burst from the seams. I swore I heard her heart hammering in her ribcage.

"Oh, it's Lindsey, Lindsey Coleman, sir. Welcome to our school and thank you for the kind introduction, Mr..." She extended her hand, trailing off as she tried not to turn on her one-hundred watt smile.

"Devlin, Mr. Devlin." He informed, gracing her with a brighter smile back. Lindsey's airy laugh sounded close to psychotic, her nervousness so apparent that it could make the blind see.

I snorted to myself at the name. His fake last name was Gaelic, meaning brave. Darington comes from daring, obviously. Daring. Brave. Hm... I wonder what genius came up with that fake name? My kiddos could have thought of something more creative, or at least more fitting, like Mr. Duckbutt. Ha! Maybe I should 'accidentally' get that started.

Lindsey moved out of the way after they finished their extended handshake, Jeremey getting closer to my shadow against the window wall. I had my arms crossed defensively, the alarms in my head blaring when I smelled his overpowering and intoxicating sandalwood scent. His eyes were foaming like the waves lapping the coastline, drinking up my image. I squeezed my arms a bit tighter, self-conscience of my Goodwill attire I was sporting today, feeling like slum compared to the women beside me and the well-dressed beast in front of me. Normally, trivial things like that, I didn't give a flying handle about, but I was outside my home turf. Jeremey was in my safe zone, my happy place, intruding, and I legally couldn't chuck tennis balls at him like in A.L.I.C.E. training. If only, if only, the woodpecker sighs.

"And would you bestow me with the honor of your name, miss?" He leaned in closer so we were eyeball-to-eyeball, his green eyes threatening to sink my blue hues into an underwater cave. What a joke he was. But, I had to be courteous; he was my boss after all . . .

Oh *Kamisama*! Back to my delusions. Simba, tally-ho, we ride! Something is rotten in the state of Denmark!

I mashed my teeth, my stare stabbing into him, but my voice was my trained professional and sugary sweet tone I've mastered, "Thank you for helping our students and staff in this transition time, Mr. Devlin. My name is Valerie Hemmingway. I'm happy to meet you." I nodded firmly, concluding our verbal exchange, lucky that his giant shadow was covering my face so my friends didn't see how cray-cray I most likely looked.

At least my voice faked it. I'm sure Playboy Don't is used to women faking it for him.

"Ah! Ms. Hemmingway, yes! I saw your achievements in the staff information packet on my desk. Very impressive for only your second year. Actually, if you don't mind, could you come meet me in my . . . I mean, the principal's office for a few minutes? I wanted to go over the agenda for this month's backpack for the hungry program and I know the chair is at a staff meeting all day. Any input you have for the meeting on Monday would be a gem."

Boy, he sounded so refined that I almost believed it. I wanted to tell him to go screw himself in the corner, but my eyes caught the held breaths of excitement of my three teaching amigas. Their expressions showed that they thought I was the heroine in a cheesy romance novel and Jeremey was Fabio. Yeah, when pigs fly. Oh wait. Better test that someday; Jeremey may have the talent to and I have a human catapult and Adam Savage on speed dial to try.

"I would be happy to assist our backpack program how I can, sir. I will be there momentarily." I bowed my head a hair and gave him a half-smile. The light in his eyes became brilliant, like I just gave him a new sports car in shiny wrapping paper. What a weirdo.

"Excellent. I will see you there soon then. Ladies, sorry for taking so much of your precious plan time, but I must be on my way. Please do not hesitate to ask me any questions. I look forward to working closely with each and every one of you. You truly are the color, life, and beauty of this building." He bowed fully at the waist, a prince that made three of the four swoon, knees fearing of caving in. I stood taller, a tower of independence. "I will see you at the meeting after school in the large conference room. Until then, I bid you all ado."

Principal Seamonkey swiveled on his heel and walked away in the same manner he had appeared, a phantom model. Christy and Lindsey chattered frantically, recounting the events of meeting Jeremey while Sherri kept complimenting on his tight ass. A vein in my neck began to throb, my fingers sore from all the self-control I had to show. I bet I had stretch marks under my dress top. A cloud of darkness was descending over my soul, the realization of all of this dawning on me like a slap from a metal, spiked glove:

Jeremey was here and at my school with an alias. That was no mistake or chance happening; this was his new O.N.J. so we could be close to work on the *monstrum* mission at all times. Jeremey was in my happy place, in charge of me and my students and their sacred futures. Jeremey now knew where I worked and could figure out where I lived, more about my personal life that I wanted no one, especially a Bringer, to know about.

Jeremey had broken into my peace, the one piece of the world that I could unwind, be myself, protect. I felt like my heart was being ripped out, vein-by-vein.

And now, I had to go meet him in my former hippie principal's office, alone, for God knows really what. There was only one thing to say as I watched my co-workers leave to their classrooms and I headed to my executioner.

"Well, damn . . ."

CHAPTER 4

Hopping Jackrabbits, I was pissed! I could feel heated rage boiling under my skin, sizzling to escape out, a volcano near eruption. My tongue was clicking against the roof of my mouth on its own, the sounds a foreign language manifested into the world to strike fear and curses. I was hexing my highly respected Chief and Mr. Stillman for keeping me in the dark about this development and forcing this mission upon me. Tunnel vision slapped on my face, a drive to make *monstrums* rue the day they were poofed into creation.

But mostly, I hated Jeremey Darington. I loathed him down from the follicles of hair attached to his scalp to the dead skin attached to the bottom of his feet, the cells, the veins, the atoms that made-up this abomination. Why did he have to be involved in my existence? He needs to run home to be the pride and joy of his poor family, not wedge his way into my life. I didn't need Hell brought to me in a suit and reeking of sandalwood and cockiness.

It took all the restraint I could muster to not stomp down the hall, my head filling with booms that collided with the explosions of thoughts in my brain. My back was plank stiff, not that of a human, but a being that would terrify my innocent lamb co-workers. Meeting with my new boss was placing myself in a ball of stress on its own. Meeting with the devil was an elevator plummeting to its final destination of a crash.

I made it to my destination, swallowing the lump in my throat as I swiveled my feet, bracing myself for the sight of seeing the breezy tie-dyed drapes, peace sign wind chimes, and wooden owl press pictures surrounding their new master, the tyrant who took over my calmness. Exhaling as much of my tension and anger as possible, having to repeat the process three full times, I turned the silver door handle, its turn sealing my forced cooperation with the beast.

Instead of the fang-baring asshole in an impeccable suit, I was greeted by Ms. Candyfield, sitting at a deep brown wooden desk in the middle of the lightly illuminated room. Her deep honey hair was piled up in her standard beehive style, clipped with a large heart decoration that matched the flowy pale pink of her top, contrasting to her baby blue skirt, and white with rainbow polka dot heels. This was her norm, her being the principal's personal secretary, her a ray of sunshine in the cloudiness of my nightmarish visions. The fact that other than her desk being moved to the middle of the room, alone, the rest of the room was as it had always been, tie-dye, owls, and windchimes.

I must have gawked longer than I thought, because I jumped when she sweetly cleared her throat, addressing my name through her cotton candy glittered lips, "Good morning Ms. Hemmingway! It is lovely to see you this morning."

Without realizing it, I curled my arms defensively into my chest, trying to make myself as small and invisible to her and the room as much as possible. Why was I acting this way? I knew it was by instinct, an automatic move, but it made no sense. And "Mr. Devlin" was nowhere to be seen.

I locked gazes with the floor before it shunned me and made me look wide-eyed with Ms. Candyfield as I chomped on one side of my lip. "Umm, it's good ... to see you too ... Umm, I'm ... I'm supposed to ... meet, I mean ... is Mr—"

"Ah yes! He mentioned one of our fine teachers was stopping by already. I am so glad everyone is getting along so well." She clapped her hands with such joy that I thought she would suddenly transform into my fairy god-mother. If only.

"The desks ..." Those two words squeaked out of my mouth, escaping from my scrambled mind, my comprehension runny.

"Mr. Devlin decided to take over to small meeting room, the door behind me on the left dear, as his office to give more space to our staff. I thought it was so kind!" She spread her arm wide to the left as she stood as if a tour guide leading me to a fascinating marvel. More like the museum of toenail clippings.

"Thank you, Ms. Candyfield. Have a good day." I bowed my head and walked past her as she gave me a dainty wave. A swell of nervousness crashed into my ribcage, threatening to capsize my stability, but I anchored my ship and dove head first into this storm that I was thrown into. I opened the door gingerly, letting it expose the contents inside slowly, the creaking making me cringe with each note it played.

I was greeted with a bare room with only a sliver of light in a corner, a wooden desk and tall shrub the sole greeters. See, being a *monstrum* hunter, I should have been smarter than I was at this moment, creeping into a dark space with no good escape route or light source, my weapons gone, my mind a puzzle with misplaced pieces. But, I stepped in anyway, my voice locked tight. I walked, right into the wolf's den I assumed was abandoned for the time.

Instead, I was near devoured.

I was fully in the room, my foot only an inch outside the door frame when the door slammed behind me and I was shoved into the wall. The force knocked the scream I was about to start out of me, the burn of the hand gripping my right forearm scalding. I heard the wall get smacked above my head, near my left ear, like a bomb went off in my skull. My reaction to drive this threat to the ground was about to kick in, but it was bound in a second by the overpowering scent of sandalwood.

Although I knew my expression was that of a shaken doe, I steeled my resolve to stare at the face that was hiding behind the door for me, behind a tall file cabinet: Jeremey.

"Welcome to my office, my little robin."

And that's why I realized he wanted to truly be moved into this office: the walls were made to be nearly sound proof for irate parents or heated staff meetings.

He arched his body closer to mine, towering, his shadow swallowing me whole. With this attempt of attack, be it as a joke or a mocking flirtation that sang in his pupils, I didn't care. All my pent up anger, confusion and questions released, an explosion so massive flying out of my body that I was afraid I would shatter.

"Get your freakin hands off me before I kick you in the balls so hard that you'll find bones in your stool! Why the bloody hell are you here anyway?"

Jeremey squeezed my forearm tighter, pinching it in a way that told me that despite the fact he was a Bringer, one who sought peaceful resolves with all races and creatures, that he had the same self-defense trainings and other techniques as a Hunter like me. He could hold me in his grasp if he wanted to and could dodge my crotch shot. His eyes bored into mine, stamping my sight with the hue of his churning sea-green eyes. There was so much depth in them, that I felt like I could dive miles in them and still learn nothing. He was as backwards as seeing an image in a mirror.

Blisters formed down my arm as he slid some of his fingers down the one he was clinging to, marking my skin with his touch, a torch, testing and teasing with how far he could reach before retracing his steps. "Maybe I'm drawn to you, a bee to nectar too sweet." He let his voice fade into a breathy whisper. I cut him off before he could continue this train of thought, derailing his tactics.

"Bull shit!" My legs began to ascend to make an impact on where the sun does not shine, but he laced his footing between my leg, ensnaring it, using the wall to pin me down even more. I was frozen in place and the only way I could kick him now was to somehow hop up for a low round-house, but then we would be in a tangled heap. I allowed him to lean me back a smidgen further, my teeth showing and snarling like an enraged Akita.

As he leaned on the hand propped against the wall, he released my arm from his hold, cupping my cheek in his hand, trailing down my cheek until it was embedded, woven soulfully into my hair. A bolt of shock coursed through me then, static in my blood petrifying me once more, but it wasn't from the feeling of being restrained; it was a drive to solve the mystery of why his touch had changed, why it was fitted with the sparks of longing in his eyes. His movements were tender.

An arrogant chuckle caught on his breath, the aroma of mint blending harmoniously with his sandalwood scent. "Oh, Ms. Hemmingway . . . we are going to have so much fun together, you working under me." His eyes danced mischievously as he slowly pushed himself off the wall to look at me head-on.

I began to rub my arms, hoping to scrub away this experience and be born anew. "In your dreams!" I retorted, snapping at him like a spoiled child. I loathed how puffed up my cheeks were, how feverish my face felt, how angry I felt towards him, like he held power over me. I glared him down as he waggled his way off of me and stepped backwards to his auburn desk chair, his tilted head matching his loopy, cocky beam. He sat down, drinking up every millimeter of my expression like I was a fine wine, the glint in his pupils as transparent to read as glass. I began trying to control my quickening, heated breath, smoldering the dragon fire that yearned to come out, but I paid the price of losing my mortal ability to speak.

After a few seconds of collection, I was able to slowly draw out a normal topic, "I assume you did not ask me here to talk about the back-pack program?"

The Joker to my Batgirl (I refuse to be a Robin, although he was a pretty delightful *Teen Titans* leader) gave me a patronizing smile, as if agreeing with a little girl's wrong answer, but showing how idiotic he thought she was in his lit-up eyes. "Like I need help forming a staple program for the district. I just wanted to chat, ask about your day, maybe take you back to my place as you rub my feet, cook me a divine meal, and for dessert—"

"Dear God, how are you fit to run this school, *any* school? I didn't realize our organizations were that desperate to have us work together. What could you possibly know about the education of these children, these little lambs that do not need to be exposed to a wolf?!"

I felt my fury spike again, peaking near my forehead under my scalp. I had to slam my fists against my legs so I would not slug at him, to not show him any more weakness than I already had. I have exposed more flaws to this creature in a suit than I ever have to anyone in three years.

He entwined his fingers and leaned on his hands, a look of wonderment spread across his face. The scholarly tone of his voice informing me that he was hiding a secret of his feelings about my word choice, my doubt in him. "You know there is more to me than meets your gorgeous eyes, my dearest." As I fumed, he stood gingerly, continuing his speech as he paced with a grace that would only be achieved by a man dressed for success as he was.

"Your Chief and Father Stillman both agreed to us working together and for me to have this O.N.J. assignment in order to be closer to your work. The threat of the bloodsucker is moving closer and his tactics are so foreign to any records of his kind that our organizations need us near each other in case we have to leave at a moment's notice and with my position, I can give you a valid excuse so your academic merit is clear." He stopped, giving me no emotion in his expression. His eyes were daring me to interrupt, a slight incline of the right side of his lip showing.

"We work for the government, *sir* . . ." I spat the final word in this train of spoken thought, "Chief or The Hunters have never had issues of getting me out of work before if need be. Plus, won't it be odd for us to leave around the same time, sort of suspicious and scandalous?" I had to clamp my mouth shut hard to not add the so needed *'moron'* as the cherry on top of my valid sundae.

"Ah, too true my whimsical little Watson, but the thing about administration is that no one can predict my schedule and I can plan investigations where we are both required to by law, by our oh so precious said government jobs, to attend. I can accommodate this snafu to where one of us leaves earlier than the other so unneeded curiosity is unlikely." He slammed his palms on his wooden desk and squared his sights on me, huskily saying with a devious twinkle and delighted smirk, "I got the power."

I gulped, stepping back to make contact with the smooth surface of the metal doorknob, wanting to cry out sanctuary when my goal was in my hand. His air was so potent that it was suffocating me and I had had enough of its toxins.

"I will recall this, my phony King." I did a mock bow, my eyebrows arched, my hand still clasping the silver knob as if it were my anchor. I was done with this conversation that went nowhere. He had an answer to every argument I had and I was no master of the debate.

His footsteps came quietly into my ears and before I could fully lift my head to flee, he grabbed my chin in a grip that was a hybrid of tender and controlling. "You better, my little robin, or I may have to punish you in the ways of my laws, for the rightful cause."

I jerked my head away, a sour face glued to my lips that contracted the popping my swift movements caused. "See you at the staff meeting after school." I hastily got out before I scurried out of his new office. I heard him holler back to me with eager excitement, his overzealous wave in my side vision when I zoomed past Ms. Candyfield. When I shut her door finally, I leaned my head on the wooden closet next door, its steadiness the only thing keeping me from falling to the floor in pieces.

I cannot deal with conversations that lead to nowhere, plans that are not crafted, promises that are not kept. Even though I can adapt and be flexible, everything has a purpose, a reason; impulse is rarely a useful skill in my world, a trait that walks dangerous waters. All I got out of this exchange was that Jeremey was my partner and I could no longer find a way around that if I wanted to protect this world from *monstrum* and no matter how much I loathed this roadblock in my life, I knew I could never give up being a Hunter.

I suppose Jeremey and I were in this mission together.

Son of a bitch!

* * *

"Welcome to my office and our refurbished community meeting room, dear staff of The Knights of Early Childhood school."

This declaration was dramatically stated by our newly appointed monarch, his Michael Kors suit framing him like the royal portrait he was practicing beaming for. All of the teachers, paraprofessionals, and afternoon support staff were in the nice and cozy meeting room, and everyone was staring at this King of Fools like he had a radiant light shining divinely out of his arrogant ass. Only myself and Coach Loom were not leaning in our seat, eating on his every word like we were a room of serfs begging for a dangling piece of molding crust. I think Coach's reasons for staying bored was the fact he had testosterone; mine was because I met the guy.

"For those lovely individuals I did not get to chat with this morning, my name is Jeremey Devlin and I have been hired by the school district to the title position of principal. I know I cannot nor do I ever expect to take the place of Mrs. Ohlinger, but I very much look forward to working with every single one of you," he paused for dramatic effect, giving each person in the room his full attention for a second, his eyes warm and thoughtful, his baby smile delightful and grateful. He really knew how to play the scene. "The purpose for today's meeting is a relaxed one. I know, how unheard of and no, I'm not insane; my mother had me tested." The room cackled at his *Big Bang Theory* and education references, scoring two points in the academic and nerdy department. I arched my eyebrows, slightly impressed and unnerved by how at ease he was with a new crowd.

"The reason I am here today is to answer questions you have regarding me or our plans for the future of this district's youngest students. And, yes, I plan to release you early, only as long as you sample one of Ms. Candyfield's cupcakes, which I hear are a state treasure." The staff nodded, zombified by the thought of cupcakes. Wow, he was charming, well-dressed, and bribing the staff with his special attention and sweet, cavity inducing treats, with a promise to get off early.

"Looks like someone has training into being a cult leader down," I mouthed heatedly under my breath.

"What did you say, honey?" I perked up and stood straighter, not realizing I was leaning into my own lap and rolling back and forth slightly in my comfy, fake leather office chair. When I heard the honey dripping in the voice that addressed me, I collected my usual innocent demeanor and glanced at Sherri. Her smile was kind, in contrast with her bold, red rose lipstick, but her eyes glinted at me as if she was trying to scan me for signs of concern, making the wink the lights caused off her glasses mix oddly.

"Oh, I was thinking about those cupcakes honestly; they *are* addicting." I held the image of a red velvet or yellow cupcake with whipped chocolate icing in a sparkly pink cupcake cup in my brain to drive my attention out of the darkness this day was causing, even if the sprinkley goodness only aided a little.

"You must be hungry. I noticed you hardly touched your food at lunch." She graced me with a look of worry and a small crease in her brow that made my chest pang with guilt. Sherri was my Momma Bear for a reason, always there to listen, care, and protect me from the harshness of normal routines, daily rituals I fought so hard to keep from her and everyone.

Before I could properly make a lame ass excuse, she interjected another comment: "Right now though, my stomach is yearning for a slice of that hunk of beef and nothing else is going to fill up my buttercup . . ." Her glasses slid and steamed slightly as she directed her full purring attention on the star of this show. I groaned, it taking all my mental strength not to hide under the desk and dig a hole to Japan.

This forced motion made me look around the room to see everyone else was abuzz with questions. The females were twittering with thrill awaiting this godly being to call on them next, waving their hands in the air in response like they were seeing the hottest rock star on the planet. It made me ill, green to the core to see, but like the twisted mind the world has given me, I knew I could not look away.

He answered each question by locking eyes and smiles with the person, bantering and jesting with ease while still sounding professional, an open book that was also mysterious. Why couldn't he be in Hollywood right now instead of here? He sure had a knack for it. Maybe Chief could make some arrangements, place him as the villain in a cop show.

"Where did you attend school, Mr. Devlin?" This endearing question came from Lindsey, who I noticed was flushed prettily, like she added more rosy blush to her China doll face. I could smell her perfume lightly from my chair three down the row. It was intoxicating and revolting at the same time, my stomach switching back and forth from butterflies to flips at what I was forced to watch.

"The University of Michigan for my Bachelors and Masters in education and Stanford to get my Ph.D in administration. They are both excellent schools and I enjoyed my time there very much."

She sighed dreamily, like she had seen a glimpse of Heaven in his melting words. I rolled my eyes mentally, beginning to ponder if Lindsay needed to be tested for craziness, like Sheldon. The poor lamb was still staring up at him, counting each millisecond he gave her the viewing of his admittedly dazzling smile, her breath getting quicker with each time she twirled the ends of her pretty dress.

Christy was behind Lindsey and raised her hand next, barely pausing for the punk to say a peep in reply, "Did you do any sort of extra-curricular activities?"

"I played football primarily when I wasn't studying or, admittedly, partying a bit with my friends. I actually went to the University of Michigan on a football scholarship my first three years. I had coaches who changed my life since sixth grade, so I knew I wanted to honor them through sports. I coached football at middle school as well at the last district I worked for. In college, I also volunteered as an ambassador to new students and liked playing other sports at leisure, like ping-pong, baseball, and track, but I sadly am not an overly creative soul, so I was not in any creative arts programs."

Figures. I sized him up hastily for a moment, his Gucci watch sparkling in the baking rays of the sun through the window. I had nothing against those who went to college on a scholarship for sports or later became coaches, but he seemed to fit the mold, the clique, and that irked my soul for some god damned unknown reason. Plus, creative arts such as singing, writing, and acting are what made me connect to others and fueled my spirit. If it was anyone else, I would have felt sorry that he never experienced the joys of them, but I never cared that I was the klutziness person in Missouri, so whatever.

Christy began to glow at his words. Her eyes were so sparkly that I could see the wheels in her head praising him turning so hard that I expected smoke to come out of her ears. Her and Lindsey caught each other's eyes and almost burst from the seams, making quite inhuman squealing noises. Sherri leaned on top of the glossy table, her large breasts taking advantage of the space, looking at Principal Preppy like she was going to have him for supper and inhale him like turkish delight. "You sound pretty impressive, Mister Man." She winked at him as her voice got lower, "Maybe you and Coach Loom could amuse us with a game of football sometime . . ."

Coach snapped up with a dazed expression at hearing his name, totally zoning out. Sweating with the attention, he wiped a bit of drool from the side of his lip. Jerk-the-not-tastic gave Coach a seriously considering look then smirked good-humoredly, giving him a nod of brotherhood before turning to address Sherri kindly. "I haven't played in a while, but if Mr. Loom would ever consider me, I would love to toss the ole' pigskin with such a fine fellow." His eyes became a clearer tone for a moment at his mock talk for Sherri, which she savored.

"Oh! I can't see you being too old there, Mr. Devlin, not enough to worry about that."

He gave a hardy chuckle, the room stilling to know the dying question of how old this miser was. I just wanted to take a nap. My weariness from not sleeping from the job the previous night after two work shifts and today's shit was taking its toll on me; even my cells felt sore to their core.

"I'm thirty-three, if you must know. My birthday is November 13th. And sure, I can keep up just fine, but I also respect my body, keeping it in shape; I never know what I have to do at a moment's notice."

Sherri shuddered in her seat as he winked at her. I was trying to pin-point a coherent sound out of a room filled to the brim with screaming with ecstasy females. His face seemed to be asking 'I wonder what beautiful loyal subject I should entertain now?' My eyes turned to slits as I tuned him out, staring at the window in my side vision and losing myself to its warmth and the illusions I needed to help me escape this pandemonium. And I almost succeeded too, until—

"Mm-hm, I am going to have to bring extra panties to work every day because this boy is going to get them a little too happy with each peek at I get at him."

And . . . I'm done.

With that, I slid my chair on its wheels away from Sherri, her too hyp-notized to notice. I was able to be ninja silent until I was against the wall, next to the window, it tempting me with a whole new world, a dazzling place I needed to know. Stupid paycheck and my little kiddos was the only thing keeping me from not busting the glass to make a getaway.

When I leaned my head back on the upper chair padding, using the wall as my backbone, my ears adjusted to tuning out all the background noise so I could rest and just hear what was needed, the dagger to my eardrums, Jeremey's *baka* voice. That jackwagon continued to answer questions about anything and everything about himself like a champ, not slowing down or sounding like he was tired. The whole room was Team Jeremey and I was Team Anyone Else (heck, even Lord Voldemort would do).

This went on for forever wrapped in an eternity until Lindsey's mousey little voice for some reason sliced the white noise in the room for me and made me register I needed to listen. "So, umm, well, Mr. Devlin . . . are you married or have any children?"

I made myself open my eyes, but kept my head down, not wanting to get out of that warm state one gets when between rest and sleep. Lindsey's question was a reasonable one, common ground, but it wasn't the question nor the fact she asked it that peaked my interest and halted my vice for a second. It was his pause, the tiniest shift of tone in the atmosphere I picked up on from Jeremey himself. It wasn't enough to be worrisome or assume he was trying to think of a lie, but it was for sure noticeable to me.

My eyes travelled up to see his face and I noticed a flicker in his eyes and how he bit his lip a fraction of a nibble. It seemed to only catch my attention. Before I could decode it and ask myself why I bothered, he answered that he was not married nor did he children as he was waiting for the right someone.

And then, he met my gaze. I took a hard intake of breath due to being spotted, moving my vision to my seat to act like I was going to rejoin the group. When I looked up three seconds, but an era later, all calm and fake collected, he had moved on, shuffling a stack of papers in his hands as he talked chipperly to Christy and Coach.

Okay Val, forget about it. This whole O.N.J. was a lie; who knew if any of this was even close to true? There was no way his college status was; I knew both those colleges were in the top five in the nation for educators and administrators and to match his image, Chief and Father Stillman probably helped the O.N.J. department with those choices. Heck if I cared he was lying, for work or otherwise. I scowled at nothing in general, my nostrils flaring at how ridiculous this all was, and went on with leaning my head back. The end of the day where I could check the reports with Kesler and hardcore beat frustration out at the gym could not get here soon enough. They sounded almost as sweet as Ms. Candyfield's cupcakes.

CHAPTER 5

It was 4:30 by the time I got to the gym at Hunter's Headquarters after finishing our meeting. The familiar doors slid open for me after I entered my passcode, fingerprint, and eye identification scans, the smell of lavender-lilac cleaning solution a comfort I wanted to snuggle in. I was home in this land of computers, data, *monstrum* images flashing, and gym and weapon equipment. I first had to debrief with Kesler on my new assignment to see what information he had for me then workout at the gym for an hour. It was a requirement we all have combat training for an hour and our own personal workout program for an hour six days a week.

In addition, I had three sessions a week with my grumpy weapons expert, one counseling session, and a staff meeting headed by Chief. It was a busy life, but as long as we didn't get any calls of an attack (oh how laughable that was), it was doable, part of this job I took such pride in.

I strode over to the cubicle area, looking for number thirty-four where my darling little Kesler would be typing away on his hip typewriter style keyboard, string cheese and Yoo-hoo at his side. I was about to turn left in the wide office lobby of headquarters to the cubicles when I noticed what appeared to be a tangle bush of fiery red hair embedded in the copier, where the compartment toners were in.

As I approached slowly with curiosity, like sneaking up on a timid animal, I heard little grunts of chippery struggle from the machine. It was adorable. I was about two feet behind the mysterious knot of locks when the person it was attached to shot up, smiling and muttering to themselves with the massive toner cylinder in hand. I had my mouth wide open, about to speak when this event occurred and had barely enough time to silently backtrack my footing and tiptoe to the start of the cubicle hall. I wasn't sure why I was being so fearful of being caught like a stalker, but apparently, I wasn't the only one spying.

When I pivoted to walk forward to my destination, I saw a strange sight: Kesler was outside his office space. He was half-hiding behind the open hallway wall, but his bright burnt orange vest with the brown checkers didn't conceal him very well. I waved at him, giving him my best friendly smile, but he didn't notice me. I soon dropped my hand gingerly, my face lighting up with recognition when I saw the darting nervousness in his eyes, the slight twitch in his white fingers gripping the wall, his mouth open as he was heavily breathing out of his reddened, sweaty face. It was hard not to beam in acknowledgement, but I felt my lips lifting upward in a the-cat-who-swallowed-the-canary grin.

"Heya Kesler . . . What're you doing?" I dragged my tone out, sounding too mischievous for my own good.

The poor lad jumped, suppressing a yelp that I could clearly see yearned to escape as he bit his tongue on the way down. I felt bad, but my chest rumbled with quiet laughter all the same. His timid green eyes bounced between me and the creature that now had a pile of paper copies. "Ms . . . Ms. Hemmingway! Oh . . . Hmm, I was just . . . well, I was supposed to be aiding the . . . the new . . . you see, the organization has a new . . ." Then he blushed and looked down hard at the glossy floor, lightly pointing his finger in the direction of the figure at the copier.

I followed his call and saw a dainty young lady in a rose-gold short jacket and sweet pleated flowy black dress, a mass of brilliantly bright red hair puffing all around her head to her slender shoulders and framing her little heart-shaped face like a mane. She was tiny, in height and size, like a doll with sprinkles of faint freckles across her nose and cheeks on her alabaster skin. As I took in her ruby rose lips and pale gold nail polish cradling the papers, she turned, smiling to herself as she happily tapped away in two inch black wedge heels, the spring in her step declaring she was overjoyed she had done a job well done with the toner crisis.

I've been there. Kudos to you, girlfriend.

I made a clicking sound, like I understood everything that was happening, but was acting unaware as I faced Kesler point blank again, leaning to lower myself closer to his level of sight. "Oh . . . I see we have a new friend. Do you know who she is, Kesler, ole' chum?"

He gulped audibly, making me lean my arm on the other side of the half-wall he was hiding behind. I felt vindictive for doing this to him, but it was too juicy and fun to see him sweat a bit, literally and figuratively.

"Oh! Hm, well . . . ," he rubbed the back of his easy-breezy copper hair anxiously, looking away from me before lifting his head up, "We have a new . . . a new intern joining us in my unit and . . . and Chief Edric wanted me to be her mentor and to show her around . . ."

I looked at where she had been moments before and arched my eyebrows, assessing the situation. "So . . . I assume you've talked to her then, eh Mr. Mentor?"

He wrung his clammy hands together, laughing shyly to himself, "Ah ha, well . . . I . . . I was about to, before I knew we had our debriefing, but . . . well, you see Ms. Hemmingway, it . . . it's like, umm—"

"I see. Well, she is a cutie pie; I'll give you that." I felt my smile widening boldly, but I wasn't sure if I was being supportive or sly.

"Yeah, she is . . . I mean! Huh?! What?!" He exclaimed, catching himself redhanded in the act. Kesler moaned like a little boy, hiding his cherry-hued face with his hands. It was too darling.

I shrugged, deciding it was time to be nice to the kid. We had interns all the time at The Hunters, those hand-selected by the government and higher-ups at the organization that saw the potential for the future success of our group. Kesler had been one of those for six months and now has worked here for a year and a half. Now, he was selected to mentor a new intern, a high honor for someone who had not hit their five years of service mark. But, I wasn't surprised; Kesler was bright, one of the best data analysts we have ever had along with being full of integrity. He was innovative, kind, and did whatever you asked with a grin, be it a nervous one, but a warm smile that tugged at your heart.

I have never seen Kesler really look at a girl, so that was a golden ray of sunshine in my life right now!

"Well, silly goose, how are you going to train her if you don't even know her name?"

"Her name is Bonnie MacKinzie. She is nineteen-years-old, a September birthday. She was born and raised in a small town near Boston, and currently is a junior at Boston University, graduating high school a year early with honors to start college at seventeen and qualified for honors and advanced placement. She has a younger sister she adores and lives with her grandmother, parents, and her sister. She enjoys basket weaving, dancing, gardening, and making jewelry when she is not solving mathematical equations. She placed top ten in the nation in every math competition and test she has ever been apart of."

I blinked, not sure how to process my surprise towards Kesler's in-depth background check of Bonnie, but I knew I should have expected it. You give Kesler a task and he will do it to a T, infinity and beyond excellence. My dazed expression was replaced with one of motherly tenderness as I stroked his cheek once then booped his nose, making him twitch like a puppy.

"Well, it seems like you got all you needed to know, except for maybe her measurements."

"Oh, well, I actually do have th—"

I held up my hand to cease his comment. "I was joking; don't be a pervert. I don't care and neither should you. Women are all special and should not be objectified. I know you went to all those trainings. Moving right along now . . ." I crossed my arms, letting my last sentences cling into the airspace, waiting to be claimed for just then, a tip-tap of two inch black heels echoed in my ears and the woman we had just been discussing came into view once more, coming close to our way. "It looks like we have a guest. Let's go introduce ourselves, Kesler."

I heard all his high-pitched wheezes and frail attempts of protests, but I grabbed his wrist loosely anyway and dragged him behind, so Bonnie would not think I was manhandling him. After a few seconds of swift walking, being dragged down by a now rigid with fear, well-dressed nerd, our red-haired maiden looked up from the file folders she was carrying to notice us. When we were close enough to have a decent conversation, I smoothly released Kesler's hand, but still pinched the cuff of his iron-pressed shirt so he could not flee. I could feel him shaking through the cotton, but I kept my tone personable and neutral as I spoke to the girl.

"Hi there. My name is Valda Hemmingway, but you can call me Valda. I am one of the huntresses of the organization." I extended my hand with a warm grin and she took it with eager excitement, but professionally, formally introducing herself to me with her job status, adding an angelic smile to match. I have small hands for a woman, but she had child's hands. In fact, even with the heels, I think she was only five feet. I was two inches taller than Kesler and he was a head taller than her. Man, I felt like a giant freak, or a tower. As long as no one was shooting flaming arrows at me . . . Wait . . .

I shook the nerdy randomness out of my noggin and Vanna White modeled my shivering friend behind me. "This is the man you want to meet, Ms. Bonnie. This is Kesler. He is my data analyst and an amazing, bright person. I am so thrilled to have him on my team. Kesler will be your mentor for your six-month internship with our Hunters organization." I side-stepped out of the way and with the hand that was still pinned to his sleeve, I practically flung him into her, him barely able to catch himself before he tripped over her.

Kesler hopped up, trying to catch his footing and breathe before staring into the face of a lovely and patient woman that would be his to guide. He bit his lip hard, then his mouth was flip-flopping open and closed back and forth like a guppy out of water.

Finally, before I wondered if I had to knock him out and give him CPR, he strutted out with his reddening face and eyes closing up, "My ... my name ... my name is ... is Kesler! Pleased ... to ... ah ... pleased to meet you!" The boy was such a wreck that he shouted the last part at the end and bowed to her, in the respectful Japanese style I gush about. I had to chomp on my lip to not snicker and have it vibrate across the whole space.

But, Ms. Bonnie didn't seem scared or stunned at all. In fact, she gave him a sweet smile, one that made her face glow from the inside out, and offered her hand to shake. Kesler looked up in amazement and beamed, taking her delicate hand in his for a moment and keeping eye contact with her honey-colored eyes.

Still spattering a bit, he kindly explained that he had a debriefing meeting with me on a code yellow situation (which means a supercritical, collaboration meeting that outsiders were not allowed to observe). She nodded slowly and waved off to deliver her file folders to the lab offices, saying she looked forward to seeing me around and working with Kesler starting tomorrow.

When she was out of sight, Kesler grinned hugely to himself, a beautiful rosy tone gracing his pale cheeks before suddenly sighing heavily. This made him cover his face with one of his hands and slumping on my shoulder a bit like an old man who had to deal with a bad leg, no cane, and talking to an annoying in-law for hours. "Well ... that was stressful."

I chuckled good-humoredly and pecked the top of his head sisterly, him accepting it as he cooled his heart rate down with the deep belly breathing our massage therapist had taught us all for stress. "Yes. A heart is a heavy burden." I looked off in the distance, feeling wise.

However, my innocent little friend didn't buy it. He gazed up at me with skepticism in his large, youthful eyes. "Is that from Studio Ghibli?" He referred to my deep quote.

"Umm... *Howl's Moving Castle*, thank you very much!" My voice leaked with offended qualities, but we both laughed and started to move over to his office. I addressed a comment he had mentioned to Bonnie earlier, ready to get in a serious, not-including-Jeremey-in-any-of-my-life-plans mode, "For our debriefing, is it really going to be just the two of us?"

He nodded firmly, a good energy coming from him that told me I may be catching a break now. "Yes. Chief figured you had too much to deal with today, adjusting to Mr. Darington at your O.N.J., so she wanted us to discuss the files and a course of action while he reads them on his own. You two will have a meeting over it sometime tomorrow. The Bringers tend to let their members read the files on their own without a group meeting or coming up with a plan later." By this point, we turned into his office and he slid into his hunter green and navy blue cushion leather chair, firing his typewriter computer back to life as I automatically went to his mini fridge to get two glass bottles of ice cold Yoo-Hoo and three sticks of mozzarella string cheese.

I hopped into the hot pink padded swivel chair next to his office space, delicately opening the drinks to serve on our "sarcasm is my second language" matching coasters and peel the string cheese to share. I knew we were going to need brain fuel. Well, at least me. "Thank *Kamisama* for that! It sucks I will have to deal with him for two jobs tomorrow, but I needed a break from him so bad. You can't even imagine Kesler how on edge I have been on all day because of his cocky nature, and I have to pretend he's my boss! I can't believe a man can be such a prick and not stab someone to death!"

I hid my face in my hands, needing some deep belly breaths myself as Kesler began to type on his machine. He tapped my back affectionately after a few seconds, making me look up, an expression of sympathy shining on his face.

I exhaled out my excess air before getting back on track, "So, any news about the *lamia* case?" As of yet, it did not have a code name, but I knew that was only a matter of time. I haven't heard from Chief all day, but I figured Kesler would be the one to have all the 4-1-1.

He took a baby mouse-sized nibble of his stringy with goodness cheese stick. Gosh golly night, he was a precious gift from above! "Chief Edric downloaded the last incident and police reports to the Cloud file for the case. I sadly have only had a little time to scan through the material, but the analysis program is highlighting key factoids for us. With our meeting time together, we should be able to see connections and map out a first course of action."

I nodded sincerely as I took another chomp of my delicious dairy delicacy, engrossed at the blazing computer screen with coding and processing I didn't understand. I talked to him through bites, "So, if I may inquire; what were you busy with?"

And in reply, or more like a confession, I had the honor of seeing this sweet boy turn flush red from his chin to his forehead in the middle of a now halted sip of Yoo-Hoo. I suppose he was doing more research on a certain cute little red-haired new assistant than I thought. I slapped his back as an attention getter after I made sure he took a hard swallow, "No worries; you're a mentor now after all and that first day takes priority—"

The computer binged just then, images and text sliding on the screen that he projected behind the screen wall with a flip switch.

The latest incident picture was of a lush field in the middle of nowhere in a star-filled night, but there was a fog rolling in the distance and what appeared to be treetop silhouettes rolling in above. A figure that was of human shape, but a mix of navy, shadow, and transparency from the grainy image, was walking slowly towards the ominous background. Stringy dark hair was plastered in dampness, side-swept to the left, but it was hard to tell any other detail since the female-looking figure was not facing the candid shot. Instead, the sensation of eerie hypnosis was in the woods, pulling into the sightless forest, and it was strong.

The headline read: "Young Local Woman Disappears In the Middle of the Night Near Camwell Forest."

The date of this disappearance stated it was only five days ago and the Camwell Forest lands were only forty miles from our present location, south of base. The article interviewed the parents, friends, and professors of this twenty-five year old grad student and other than working late night shifts sometimes at the on-campus cyber cafe, she was a role model, good person, and went straight home after curfew. The odd thing was that this girl was clearly not in a vest or apron, but a dress, or at least in a flowing skirt. And the last place that she was seen was leaving the cafe, but her car was at her parent's house and the keys in their usual entry hall bowl, according to the reports from her boss, the security cameras outside the school cafe, and her parents.

Kesler recorded the data into the mission's database, including locations, times, and any scrap of information about this young lady's report, seeing if it matched with police findings. We moved on to the two next most recent articles: a forty-two year old insurance salesman from Kansas City three weeks ago and a single mother in her early thirties with bouncy blonde hair as vibrant as the California waves she lived by until her disappearance a month before. These images had much more blurry surroundings than the grad student's article, but we were able to clearly see a downtown cityscape in the gentleman's and a sandy beach with lush waves by a pier in California. However, the 'dots' that we assumed were people hardly gave us any clues.

As Kesler dragged and dropped files, highlighting every location and number he could muster, we discussed any connections we could find, but it was like grabbing for straws in the middle of the ocean. I rested my elbows on my lap and rested my chin in my hands, trying to relax as I pieced together this mystical mystery, this puzzle that had others' lives on the line.

"This doesn't make any sense," I hoarsely voiced, "none of the ages, social classes, locations, sizes, interests, blood types . . . *Nothing* really adds up." I tapped my finger against my chin in a dull rhythm, trying to block out the white noise in my head. "Unless the *monstrum* is hungry at these times, which as a *lamia* is possible, or he is just so full of malice, willing to break the contract we have with the *lamia* clan, it doesn't any sense. Usually in modern *lamia* cases, the victims are alone with no one around, not hypnotized to be dragged off to become a snack."

I huffed out excess air that was locked tight in my chest. "All the cases report that the last time each person was seen was after midnight, which screams creepy *monstrum* clique. That does not give us much; we do most of our hunting at night, as you are aware. Each area is also near a wooded area. The grad student was three miles from her house to the forest, the agent had a park trail a mile off the highway near his office, and the mother had a driftwood and sand wasteland four miles off the main pier of the beach. Those areas do seem like perfect locations to hypnotize humans from a distance, luring them into the coverage of trees and the night. But . . ." I bit my lip, trying not to let my gears of fear spiral out of control and smoke, "if they can project their abilities that far or hold them in their clutches for that long of a time . . ."

Kesler and I locked gazes, his mind syncing with mine, but we kept our final statement to ourselves. "I'll keep working on finding connections between all the cases we have documents on and see if there is a pattern in the locations. It does seem to be moving from west to east." He went into full on all-star analyst mode, typing at the speed of sound, the colors and downloading of data reflecting boldly in his doe pupils. He sipped the last swig of his Yoo-hoo and without looking at me, said, "Plus, I believe it is time for your independent workout session."

I threw my head back overdramatically, flopping my hair over the back of my chair as I groaned loudly, but it was just partly for show. "Gah!" I smacked my forehead, "Here I had to have a super long work-out session with Captain Prudy-Pants this morning in self-defense and weapons training because, quote, I am a 'chocolate tart snark,' but I suppose an hour of gym time won't kill me." Kesler gave me a sideways smirk that made him actually look his age. If he could keep that glance with Ms. Bonnie, he might become the hottest math nerd in this cubicle hallway.

I gradually propped myself up out of the chair, it creaking like my back. Dang, I feel like an old person! "Whelp, time to destress-with sweat! That should be our gym slogan!" We both chuckled briefly at this as Kesler returned to his research.

"I'll email you the mission's key factoids the database finds after I give it a second check before I leave tonight. I know you'll need them for your meeting with Mr. Darington tomorrow."

"ARGH!" This one was legit agony, but I let out the tension with a few tango stomps on the tile. Olay! I ended in a ungraceful twirl and a double clap before landing to peck Kesler on the cheek lightly. "Thanks for the reminder, but you make sure you tell Ms. Bonnie when she can go home, All Mighty Mentor." I skipped out of the room, the last sound I heard in the hallway was Kesler's thudding heartbeat against his rib cage and incoherent babbles.

* * *

I emerged from the girl's locker room feeling pumped, hoping that the stretch of my muscles would allow my mind to go into a state of calm. I went up the stairs to the workout area, rounding the narrow corner to the sliding door that required my thumbprint and passcode. When I gained permission to proceed, I unslung my pink High School Musical gym bag (Zac Efron is yummy; don't judge me) to place it in the corner of the room by the water fountain so I could see it, throwing my purple fluffy towel on top.

After a swig of water from my *Mighty Morphin Power Rangers* bottle, I zoomed past the mirror to get a glimpse of my reflection. From here, I looked like an overly tired girl with bruised circles under her eyes, little dots and lines on her arms from fights, roadmaps to an adventure to a land mortals didn't know. I graced a messy ponytail, an old, dull, gray "Baton

Twirling Team" shirt and hot pink workout capris. I was a mismatched specimen with my youth and battering, wise in eyes, young in soul, but my spirit, like my pale image staring back at me, it felt lost at times. I had a roaring sense of justice, a creative essence, a determination to survive and wanted to have some playful fun while doing it. That doesn't mean it always reached my heart. My heart is on standby and I wasn't sure it would ever fully restart again.

I ventured over to the chest fly machine, testing out the rhyme I wanted to pace myself at. I was alone, which was a needed blessing, and a rarity. I was getting into a slow momentum, the quiet humming of the AC for once sending me in a trance when I heard the gentle whoosh of the sliding door. Well, my two minutes of solitude was nice, but, as a kindergarten teacher, I knew how to be a good sharer and at least I can put my IPod earbuds in.

Until I saw who entered the room. Scratch that; I refuse to share anything with the devil.

My mind was immediately on alert, but my body refused to accept reality in a timely manner, letting go of the handles with a strain, like I was heavy. I could feel my hard glare sinking my eyeballs into my skull, my mouth pouting and face too hot. When the machine finally gave way to allow me to move my limbs freely, I leaned forward, ready to challenge this foe that was wearing way too much aftershave, bright red athletic shorts, and a *tight* cobalt blue Puma brand athletic shirt.

Through clenched teeth, I addressed the elephant in the room as he grinned at me like a monkey finding a hidden banana, "What... the hell... are you...?"

"Ms... Ms Hemming... way...!" A voice crackled the air like a firecracker in the humid air. In the doorway, screeching to a sudden halt with his wingspan frantic, face panting and hot, was my Kesler, his mouth agape, the personification of terrified. The three of us all locked gazes for what passed like an eternity, the tension too crisp for me, but Stupid Buttmunch was at ease, arching his eyebrow confused at my friend and flirty at me. He's lucky I'm sitting...

"Umm ... Ms Hemmingway, I ... I'm sorry to intrude, but ... I just found out ... about—" his sights shifted timidly to the intruder to our compound, who looked monstrous compared to Kesler's little frame, his body getting swallowed by the shadow. Kesler's lip trembled before he found his breathy voice again, "But ... I see ... I see you discovered ... what I just did when ... you, ah ... left ..." Then he did a little bow after leaning on the glass, his forehead leaving a sweat print, a reminder of him before he bolted in near tears.

Then, we were alone, Jeremey and me.

He placed his hands dramatically on his hips and gave me a look of oozing confidence. It made me feel sick in the pit of my stomach. Showing me his pearly whites, he strode over to the free weights, pretending to take his time and hover over the massively heavy ones. I resisted the urge to huff and mock how casually he appeared to workout while I was still on fifteen pound weights, but my form was excellent. Plus, I knew how to handle all my weapons like the licensed pro I was. So, hardy-har-har to you, annoying sir!

I bent down to get out my pink and lime green free weights to start my curl routine on the bench. The tension and slight burn in my muscles felt reassuring, empowering me, but the stinging heat that was creeping in my cheeks from the start of sweat and stress was beyond flustering. Jeremey started to make grunting sounds, daring me to look up at him. He gave me a look that showed he was pretending he wasn't interested in my whole attention, but he secretly was yearning for it. His cheeks puffed out with a victorious intake as he curled a, sad to admit, impressive weighted dumb-bell. When he caught sight of my quick glance, his glass green eyes winked at me, a childish sparkle that got my breathing raspy.

After he slammed the weights down, right before I was done with my count, I squared my jaw and asked him point blank, tired of this charade, "Okay Jeremey, what the hell are you doing working out, without consent, in The Hunters' gym?" My teeth mashed together at the same time I pounded my fist angrily into the side of my pants, causing a clashing friction duet.

His response? He stretched before gracing me with a full smile of white teeth, while positioning himself to do some leg stretches right in front of my mat area, blocking my plan to go to a new machine. "Well, Chief Edric and Father Stillman approached me when I clocked in this afternoon. I believe you were in a research meeting with that frightened little hobbit of a fellow, Chandler—"

"Kesler!" I defended my dear friend, huffing out my annoyance with the turn of my head.

Beef Jerky Jerk just shrugged and did some sit-ups as he continued his explanation, "Well, our bosses were showing me around the Central Computer room and let me analyze the same articles you guys were. Father then suggested that since your headquarters was closer to all of the most recent crime scenes, then it would make sense for me to report to work here on this joint assignment. Like you, my sweet, tasty honeydew, I have a routine of combat training, self-defense, counselling, meetings, research conducting, and work-outs I cannot, for my delicate as a flower mental health, alter or skip for such a long period of time. HA! Lady Edric looked like she swallowed a moldy peach pit when Father Stillman brought it up, but somehow, the geezer wore her down. He has so much skill that it makes me almost want to buy me some dopey, Mr. Rogers inspired sweater vests. Almost . . ."

He hooted at the memory of my Chief, my tough as nails, and does it with grace while her nose is it the air Chief, succumbing to a middle aged man only because he had a kind voice and innocent smile that made him the dream casting for a preschool educational program T.V. host!

I would have to do some probing with Chief once Bozo the Spiked Clown was gone for the night. Where was my life heading? I thought the agency was my safe haven from the outside judgements and worries of the world. Yes, I get I am supposed to be outside, saving the lives and innocence of America's citizens, but whatever! The glass can be looked at in many angles.

I braced myself, feeling that I aged fifty years in my lower back, careful not to make direct eye contact as I snubbed my way around his shifting position. "I see. Well, for this evening, how nice for you. But, let me tell you now, *sir . . .*" I hissed my mock of his fake superiority over me, "you are *not* a Hunter, so you must respect and abide by our regulations, including not bothering an agent during their workout session. Often, these are the few calming moments we have."

I didn't give him a chance to reply to my snippy, but informally informative tone, seeking and claiming the treadmill that was my self-proclaimed spot. I would have liked to turn the T.V. on and watch a classic show from T.V. Land or one of the music stations since I was for once alone from my fellow Hunters, but I had to close myself off again because Tight Ass (in more ways than one I was noticing as he bent to touch his toes) was here. Oh well. I suppose being locked inside my soul through my earbuds and the pulse of the melodies of my liking was the next step.

I programmed my pace, started the heart monitor controls, and took my first steps, on my way on this journey around a make-believe track. My ears began absorbing the rhythms and lyrics with the beat of my strides. I was almost fully engrossed in the Val Zone, but then I saw Jack Stupidington take the machine to my right. He stapled a baboon grin to his face as he pressed the buttons to start matching my fast walk. I rolled my eyes and stared straight ahead, ignoring him, focusing on the road I had to travel that only I could tread.

To respect the confines of this space, I had my music on a low volume, a habit of good human nature that I did on autopilot. I expected Jock the Cock to do the same, but alas, I was disappointed. The first thing I noticed was the flashing of colors in front of my eyes as the T.V. was turned on. Okay, whatever. Most people in the gym use the subtitles to not bug the other people. I heard him "hmming" to himself and bulging his tongue on the insides of his cheek to make it expand humorously as he thought while channel surfing, searching for the wave that would ride him to the climax of this workout.

I inhaled and then exhaled trying to find another cleansing breath to become one with this Panic of the Disco song I recently just downloaded when instead, I heard a blaring line of a song I never expected to hear in a *monstrum* hunting killing establishment:

"Everybody makes mistakes . . ."

I jolted upright, losing my right earbud in the process as I tried to regain my balance of almost sliding off the treadmill, my lungs and heart jumping up into my throat. It took me a moment or two to carefully baby step back into my power walk pace, for suddenly, as my dad would elegantly inform, the track felt as slick as greased cow poop.

"Oh gosh, yes! It's Hannah Montana! I freakin' love her! This is my jam!" These fangirling exclaims came from Jeremey to my right, who was cooing with his curled hands under his chin, his eyes dazzling to reflect the rosy image he was witnessing on the flat screen. With a flare that would have popped my head off if I was next to him, he thrusted his arms widely outward to the ceiling, wooting with glee. He continued to jog slowly on, but with passion that could run a power factory.

I use the expression 'mind blown' like everyone else, but that is what was going on. Let me tell you, having your brain so shocked that it cannot process what it is seeing as it slowly melts into your socks is a scary thing we should not joke about any longer. Watching Jeremey flip his luscious fake locks and use an invisible sparkling microphone to get his imaginary fans to cheer his name was sickening. I would much rather be licking salt off of sandpaper.

"Nobody's Perfect! I gotta work it! Again and again til I get it right. Sing with me, darling!" Jeremey proclaimed as he shook his hips with too much pizzazz.

My ears could not handle the belting out of his inner divo and I cringed, my arms wrapping around myself. I just wanted to sink into the corner into the shadows and forget about the expensive therapy I was now going to require. I'll send a bill from the Underworld.

"What... is wrong... with you?" My voice cracked, a dry, wispy whisper as I somehow kept my stance afloat on the treadmill.

He cocked his head towards me and gave a bemused, boyish smile with no shame in my direction. "Don't you see what a goddess Hannah is? Her energy, her message, is empowering to me. What's wrong with wanting to soak that up?" His eyes were kind and dead serious as they bore into mine, a connection sizzling between us for the longest second ever until I was burned and looked away.

What was I supposed to say to that? I know what it's like to be picked on for liking something uncool that fills your soul with glee (*Glee*, the show being one of those things). I was just stunned to see him act so imperfect yet innocent. I didn't agree with his choice in cult following songs, but who was I to judge?

"Plus, the music totally rocks my nipples until they harden! Among other things, my lady... I LOVE YOU HANNAH!" At his declaration of love he hollered so even the angels were ducking from the noise, he took his hand towel from the treadmill carrier and swung it over his head rapidly, a raging hormonal man-boy!

And with that, I was done. With no emotion left in my body, I turned off my treadmill with ease, my towel draped over me. I grabbed my duffle bag in an almost robotic like state. I nonchalantly exited the gym, the clear sliding door the only sound I could process. The last utterances I heard but refused to acknowledge was Duck Face McButtMuffin wailing into a power ballad and then made the sound of what appeared to be a sloppy kissing smack, yelling, "I will serenade you once more when we meet again, my honey bunny love!"

The door closed behind me, a clear exit to this new, unexpected chapter in the horror novel I lived in. I strode forward, steam coming out of my nostrils, a method of composure that took much of my energy. The halls glided past me, the shadows elongating into stripes that seemed to slowly bend to my whim, as if they were drooping with sorrow for me. My essence was drained and I felt like a husk.

Maybe, I was the one who would be slain if I was not careful.

CHAPTER 6

"And that is why, I think personally, that grabbing the nuts and twisting them like a warm, buttery, German pretzel would be the best method. The end."

The irritation in my tone could almost be seen bouncing off the ceiling, clashing with the ticking of the glaringly vibrant, yellow clock. The abundance of plant life made the outline of my vision fuzzy, as if I was a dull square in a land of poppin, forest-toned hues. And yet, the atmosphere around me was untwisting the knots in my guts, keeping the churning anger inside me small and trapped. That was thanks to the sophisticated and pleasant woman in her teal and navy blazer and pencil skirt, sitting in a lush forest green chair. This wave of calm allowed my eyes to rest as if I was a bird flying across the sea and found an island to perch on.

"Well, you know I can ask you the stereotypical, annoying question of 'how does that make you feel,' but with only ten minutes left in our session, who has the time or yearning for that?" Amy Bruckman's light brown eyes made you feel fuzzy inside with comfort like you were totally safe, her rich voice sounding like church bells when she laughed.

That is what got her into this position: her voice, or more like the power compelled by her words. She was a *kotodama*, a psychic gifted with the ability to use her words to do many things. In her position as The

Hunters shrink and case manager, she used her skills to allow her patients to calm down, feel relaxed enough to reveal repressed feelings that are harming them, to help them sleep, and other traits along these lines. It is not hypnosis; more like she can pull out or numb feelings or memories to help you. The coolest thing I have seen her do was open locked doors, freeze animated corpses, and made someone float off a twenty story ledge when he almost jumped to commit suicide, all with her words alone.

Her abilities are remarkable. So much so that she is forced to wear a navy blue circular hair clip on the left side of her head. It, however, has a dual purpose: it tracks her brain waves at all times in our system to make sure she will not use her powers to hurt us. I know she will never do that and it almost insults me as a professional that our organization would do this, but, some in The Hunters classify her as a *monstrum*, a freak, due to her gifts. In the world I am forced to tackle, *monstrum* who look and act human are, indeed, the scariest of all, but Amy is not like that. Still, she smiles and faces the paranoia thrown at her, the glances and fear she has encountered her entire life for being truly gifted.

It honestly made me sick in my stomach to think about how we treated one of our own and it was near impossible to swallow when I heard people address her as a *monstrum*.

Pulling myself back into reality and the warmth from our session's aura, I draped my arm with zest over my forehead to reply to her clique question. I turned away like I was a Southern peach in a *Gone with the Wind* knock-off, me adding the accent as an accessory to match, "Well, I do declare, that would be worse than a piglet in a patch full of clover with buzzing bees zipping around his plump rump." When I opened one of my eyes to peer at her reaction, I was graced with an elegant chuckle from my friend and I joined in the melodious spell.

"Well, honestly," Amy crossed her legs and folded her hands gracefully in her lap. "Your dislike for Mr. Jeremey is very apparent. Yet I know how loyal you are to our organization and your missions. Ms. Edric wouldn't have made this decision lightly."

"Yeah, I understand that." I sighed out.

She cocked her head. The aura around me shifted slightly, like someone was studying you from afar. I recognized this projection she was emitting; Amy was trying to keep my mind steady, logical, so she could get a clear reading on my thoughts, how I felt about this situation without emotions interfering too much. I called it the Spock Method.

"Call it blasphemy if you like, but you and The Bringers all have common ground. Both organizations came from the first monster research organization our forefathers founded. Even now, both have the job to protect mankind from the *monstrum*, even if your methods of doing so differ. With that mindset, I think you can at least work with Mr. Darington to help make sure there are no more missing person cases. Besides," she cupped her chin and gave me a sly expression, the aura gaining a bit of a sharp edge of impish nature, "you can always come and complain to me. I adore your whimsical outlook on life."

I mumbled, my cheeks expanding outward like a pufferfish, "I know . . ." Damn her and her level-headed way of thinking!

"Now, tell me about your little ones, the precious kitty I am going to steal from you someday, and the latest Japanese craze you are fangirling over? You know I live through your exploits!" This got a chuckle out of both of us as I sat up and curled my knees into myself on the comfy bench.

"Well, my students are working on basic addition, what causes motion, and writing their middle names. Socks is my princess and I will skin anyone who tries to harm her and you know as well as I do I am certified to do this, quickly too. I currently am watching the newest Type Moon anime series, replaying the *Kingdom Hearts* games in HD, and reading a romantic dramedy manga set in the Edo period. And that's all going in the small duplex world of Valda Hemmingway. Now you can bask in the light of my weirdness."

I stood up, hearing the timer go off for our session. "You gonna be online tonight?" I inquired as I fixed the insole of my shoe.

Amy crossed her arms and gave me a warming smile. "Well, we do have a riveting game of Words with Friends to play."

I thanked her and gave her a gentle tap on the shoulder. "Take care of yourself."

The atmosphere around me glistened, beginning to change back to normal. The emotions I had to deal with slowly resurfaced into my chest. My hand hovered an inch from the door handle and then twitched, not quite ready to turn. "Umm...Amy...?"

"Hm?"

"Have you...I mean, what...what should I do...if I can't handle this?" My voice felt like it was lost in fog, going down into a deep tunnel. Doubt was seeping into my bones.

Her eyes became tender and compassionate, a nonverbal understanding passing through us. "Girl, you are the most dedicated member of this organization. You have an admirable work ethic and fine-tuned skills. I know this will be a challenge, but for you, it will be just another notch in your accomplishment belt. And you have plenty of support. Just see Mr. Darington as a goofy, overly cologned teammate for the fight against the *monstrums*. You know, when he is not partying too hard in his own gelled head."

I nodded, giggling at her words and excellent description. I waved then and exited, my gut throbbing with guilt, a guilt that did not want to quiet. One word was screaming in my head: *Fraud.*

What scared me the most, a shock that sprang up from nowhere, was that I wasn't sure if this message was for Jeremey, or myself.

* * *

My hand slid down to find the trigger of the beautifully embroidered, late 1800s holy silver gun, the small machine of destruction giving me the hope to bring light back into the world. My reflexes had to be quick for this opponent could slice through the air like it was nothing. As the creature's antlers came crashing a mere inch above my head, instead of scraping the steel storage box I was trying to seek cover behind, I pushed myself into a dodge roll. My reward? First, a lovely scrape on my left elbow. Second, my ears bleeding from the enraged screeching of the flying bloody beastie in the storage simulation room. These prizes were rip-offs.

"You damn little Easter knock off!"

I plastered my body against an old Bobcat, positioning my gun in a crouched police stake-off position. I heard its bubbling hiss echo across the metallic room, the *monstrum* creating a gust as it swooped down past me, barely missing because of the close proximity of the shelves next to me. This annoying little guy was getting on my last nerve.

I'm seriously rethinking the second I volunteered for the science department to help them with this experiment of releasing a captured *monstrum* to see the full extent of its abilities in a caged area before his execution. Curse my loving heart.

The Wolpertinger let out a bellow of insanity, only allowing me to duck a split second before its dive. Sadly, I lost a few hairs in the process from the top of my head. Oh no it didn't!

This fluffy, antlered bastard is going down!

The hanging lights shivered with each beat of its wings, following the tempo of my adrenaline. At this rate, the little whirlwind was going to trash the storage room and although the walls could change backgrounds with matching stimulus, a portion of the supplies are the genuine articles. I craned my neck upward to get a look at it and our gazes locked, its golden eyes giving me a glisten of fury and hunger, I its soul target.

"Well, looks like our dance is over."

In one lightning motion, I stood up to my full height, this causing the Wolpertinger to swoop with dashing speed right at me: face, fur, fangs, antlers, and all. Locking onto this *monstrum* with a keen eye and my target capture device, I aimed and took a shot: "Our game is over!"

With that, the bullet blasted out of the gun's barrel, soaring at the perfect angle, colliding with the face of the creature to stun it, but it was not enough to slow down its pursuit. That's fine; I believe in fairness with a warning shot. Once more, I aimed and let the bullet fly, this time the ammo landing straight into its snout and exploding in a shower of blood-charred fur, and chipped away bone pieces, soaking me in a rain of literal bloody victory.

"*Monstrum* of Wolpertinger classification exterminated. Data and recording saved. Sprinkler cleansing system activation commencing."

With this announcement by Scriba, sort of like our version of a super-powered Siri, the sprinklers doused me in steaming warm water to wash off most of the gunk in the room. Scriba's robot hand grabbed the carcass of the beast and slid it into a containment box in an automatic floorboard along with a chunk of antler, decent sized tuft of fur, a tooth, and a few desert sand-toned feathers. The science team will take a closer look at the anatomy of the Wolpertinger, one that happened to be a male leader. This jackalope-sized hare with massive and near griffon like wings is an invasive species, thriving on murdering desert creatures and attacking human travelers for no reason. They have a blood lust and are way too speedy for their own good, hence why we had to capture one instead of annihilating it in the open skies of the Sahara.

I looked towards the Plexiglas slot at the top of the high entry wall and gave a thumbs-up so Bill from Science could let me out through the secret door in the back to get cleaned up. The ping and unhinging of the steel door happened a second later and I ventured to the passageway to one of our many decontamination rooms. I took a gander at the wall clock. "Let's see. It's 6:37. I have time for a quick shower and change of clothes. I don't have duty today, so as long as I get there around 7:45, I will be good. I'm so glad I did my lesson plans last night and I already got my workout in before the experiment..." I mumbled this as I got into a steaming, welcoming shower, scrubbing with the clinical honey soap to get toxins off of my skin. I lathered up, regaining my humanity back from my fighter rush, the vapor sinking into my pores.

After drying off, I slipped into my purple striped shirt and matching cardigan with some black dress slacks, tying my hair back into a loose bun so it could air dry on the way to work. My locks take forever to dry. I felt much better, like I had been reborn and was ready to face the world, to embrace the good in my youthful, smiling students. One step forward! I so needed a good killing and warm antiseptic shower—

"Awww, I missed the yummy rub-a-dub-dub, my beauty with the booty in the tub. How I will regret this the rest of the day!"

"Ahhh!" An unwarrior shriek escaped my lips, causing my collected lesson plan book and planner to crash onto the tile. I stood there frozen, staring into the sea-green glistening eyes of the dink of dolts, Darington, leaning all causally over the tall counter in the third floor locker room opening. He was styling in a deep plum purple Ralph Lauren suit and red and ivory checkered vest and tie (most likely both silk). Almighty Mandles, this was only his sixth day as our principal for the organization's cover-up assignment and every day, he wears a different suit set that costs probably twice my monthly car payment.

I stared him down once I picked up my materials, my gaze never leaving his. His irises churned like rolling waves of green water and yet his hair was so stiff from gel I wasn't sure a level three hurricane could move it. Trying to hide my semi-rigid breath, I inhaled out, "What the Donald Duck are you doing here, you jerk water?"

He nibbled his lip, but it could not suppress his cat-ate-the-canary grin. "Starting early with the naughty language, my dear? Maybe I should paddle you . . ."

"Shut up! Seriously, how'd the beef wellington did you get through the clearance? And FYI: I am prepping for my kindergarten classroom mindset like I do each morning." I grumbled the last sentence, not able to make full eye contact with the slimy snake. Not like I care what he thinks, but the facade of him being my boss (gag me) takes practice.

"Well, my little robin, whilst I am on this mission co-created by both our groups, I have a temporary code to most of the facilities as long as I abide to the confidentiality agreement I signed, a procedure I am used to between The Bringers and working at schools." He draped his arm on a tall stool chair that was behind him, looking like a spokesmodel for those classy rich men that drink bottles of $8 wine like it's what James Bond does to lay all the chicks who end up betraying him. "I heard you do early morning trainings and I wanted to join you with the fine, rustic gentlemen that barks like a throaty crocodile, but you were gone by then. Props for getting up at the crack of dawn. Anywho, I ran into Lizzie in the Science Department. We shared a cinnamon bagel and black coffee. She is a delight and in our stimulating conversation, she informed me you volunteered for an experiment. Very noble of you."

A rattly sigh escaped my mouth as I gave a concealing smile. Lizzie was a lovely frizzy red-headed beauty that made science her lover, but I suppose I underestimated Jeremey's dicky charms. I would have to correct her later. "Surprised you're praising me since our ideals are so different . . ." A tingle of victory of annoying this dogapus filled my chest.

He looked downward at his blindingly shined Allen Edmonds shoes, a grumpy pout on his lips for a few seconds before he turned slowly to answer me, "The massacre of a creature after you captured it from his home is inhumane, especially when your goal was to gain data. You know The Bringers have the most thorough and state-of-the-art technologies and methods for obtaining information. I am not even sure why you guys need a research team when you murder in cold blood."

Anger steamed within me and expelled out like the smoke of an active volcano. "We need the research so we can understand how to save lives. Yes, it was inhumane to kill that *monstrum*, because none of them are human! By understanding each *monstrum*, we know how to track it, its origin so we know what weapons to use, how to defend society against it, how to save innocents. I understand it is a creature and survival is its instinct, but The Hunters are following ours as well, to protect ourselves. An area of the Sahara was flooded with random attacks by a creature no one could see, children even losing limbs and the wildlife dead for sixty miles. The

Wolpertinger was being invasive and we had to do something to stop the fear and suspicion along with the chaos. Besides, you guys may have the better data tools, but it's not like you'd ever in Hell share them with us!"

As my fists trembled, I saw his face relax and his eyes looked sympathetic, like I was a little girl who didn't understand real world problems. I knew he was an old fart, but that haze in his expression was pissing me off. Lord, I wanted to punch it off him!

"And you guys would never share weapon information with us, so we are at an eternal impasse it seems."

"Like you'd ever want it, the way you guys act like hippies!" My tone was quiet, but it rang through the hallow hall. The clock was chiming, too cheery sounding for this twisted conversation. I knew we could never agree, so what was the point in all of this? I could find this bastard/bitch bloodsucking human snatcher myself or with another agent. I steeled my gaze against him and took a few steps forward, already later than I wanted to be to get to my longish drive to school. If I got clearance, I may be able to take my motorcycle and have someone drop my Kia Rio off in the parking lot and switch them out.

Jerk the Turd stood then, his movement smooth and graceful, showing the close-cut of his suit. I tried not to notice the impeccable fit that Tim Gunn would be proud of. "At least we share the evil protection spray. Just to let you know, it still smells pretty strong on you. I know you were trying to rush to embrace your youngsters and jump into my arms, but you might want to use a spritz or two more of your trademark cherry blossom mist." The smile he gave me was one that was slightly warm and worried, which if I wasn't so steamed would have made me trip from the shock factor alone. "I'll see you at school." I heard him utter as I exited the locker room. I will only get about 40 minutes of peace from him, but with each click of my dress shoes, I stomped out the irritation he placed under my skin and replaced it with the knowledge that my experiment will save lives.

That is what it's all about.

* * *

"So, how did you spill the maple syrup on you again?" Lindsey's singsong voice became flat with baffled inquisitiveness, her dainty yellow fork being held flippedly in her hand, like it doubted me too.

Although I tried to stay tall, my shoulders were hunching over to shield myself. A chopstick full of white rice dangled in the air as I stared at the space off behind Lindsey's head in the staff room during lunch. "Well, I took longer than I thought on my walk and I forgot to scrub off my bug spray. So, I crammed a piece of my Eggo waffles in my mouth as I leaned over my counter, and the syrup from my dip tipped over on my plate. I . . . being the clean freak I am, I tried to catch it and instead, it ended up all over my arms. I tried to clean it up with soap, but I guess I didn't do such a bang-up job."

A nervous chuckle escaped my mouth and my hand started smoothing the back of my hair. I was able to nibble my rice, going next for one of my octopus wieners, the sight of my pink and blue *Kiki's Delivery Service* bento box cheering me up with its *kawaii* characters and blossoms.

Unfortunately for me, Captain Dumbass was right; my *Malum Praesidium* spray wasn't washed off all the way. *Malum Praesidium,* evil protection spray, is like sunscreen, where it cannot stop *monstrum* attacking us, however if they make contact with our skin, it will not break it. Sadly, some *monstrum* are created this way: a scratch, a bite, or such like that. That's the worst case scenario. *Monstrum* marks can make humans extremely ill or even cause a slow death. So, it's like we are wearing a light layer of invisible clothes with the spray to protect us. The spray smells like strong bug spray and maple syrup mixed, hence the confusion with my aroma today.

"You need to stop taking these early morning walks, darling, if you are that delicate to bugs that you have to wear such strong spray before the sun is even awake." Sherri sliced a piece of her steak fillet and dipped it and a potato chuck in savory smelling sauce, an Irish recipe she had been working on perfecting. Momma Bear knew her way around the kitchen.

"Ha . . . maybe you're right . . ." My appetite was fading, like my confidence in balancing both lives. I wonder how Kim Possible did it sometimes.

It really was tiring. But, not enough that I would ever let Jeremey the Horny, but Lonely Reindeer know about it.

Christy had lunch duty with the kiddos that day sadly, but we still kept up a lively conversation about our upcoming quarter assessment over shapes, how our first sight word practices were going, and the latest episodes of the popular Netflix shows. I knew enough from the Internet to follow along, but I keep up with the anime, not the mainstream stuff. In the blink of an eye it seemed, lunch was over and we had to pick-up our students. My *hoshis* had a bathroom break and then gym today. We rushed off to the races to get them to P.E. on time. Once Alivia shut the door for Coach, I let out a sigh of relief, eager to start my plan period of grading, sorting centers, and reviewing a newly updated IEP, or maybe take a nap. I will let my body decide what I could handle.

"Hey, sweet cheeks. Heading my way?"

I knew that annoying tone anywhere, like a fly you just can't seem to swat, and my eyes were as deadly as the stinger of his cousin the bee.

Through gritted teeth, I asked him, "Je—oh, Mr. Delvin. It is . . . a pleasure to see you . . . *sir*. What can I do for you today?"

Dog-on-Chicken gave me a sugary smile that hurt my teeth and made me want to break his. I'd even be willing to pay his dental bill. "A delight to see you Ms. Hemmingway. Do you have a moment? I want to discuss an excellent observation I saw you do this morning . . ."

Before I could 'kindly' decline, he grabbed my elbow and led me to the rail by the window in the middle of our special class hall. It took all my strength not to allow my Hunter's self-defense training to kick in and break his nose. It would have been so easy to do! I prayed that someone would come save me, but the hallway on both sides was dead clear. Son of a batch of cookies!

"Look, *Mr. Devlin*, I really don't have time to—"

"There's been another *lamia* incident." And with that whisper, chills ran down my spine. Time seemed to stop around us. The rustling of the leaves in the trees settled, the air stilling, and the colors of the hall muting to a dull amber.

My instincts flared up, my mind sharp and calm to learn the details. My muscles became tight and warm, prepared to go in for the kill. "You got a report from Mr. Stillman?"

His nod in reply was somber. "Yes. Father Stillman contacted me about fifteen minutes ago. I wanted to wait until I knew you were on your plan period. It's nice to know where you are at all times during the school day."

I puffed some irritated air in his direction, showing my disapproval. "That's more of a reason for me to have pepper spray in my pocket for you at all times. And shouldn't we be discussing this in your oh so fancy chamber of silence?" I crossed my arms to lean against the window.

"The superintendent is running a meeting in there with some important investors about an addition to the building next year and Ms. Candyfloss is working in her office. And it takes more than some spray to exterminate me, precious flower." His eyes had a glint of flirtation in them, our conflict from this morning no longer outwardly lingering with him. I pushed it down into the depths of my stomach, for now.

Jerking-Off-Too-Much continued, "Regardless, Chief Edric got a report from an informant of some suspicious activity the past two weeks or so at a Mexican goth dance club in Springfield. About six young people have mysteriously disappeared, seemingly leaving the club in a daze and random fog appearing behind them once they exited the building. However, the patrons by the wanderers seem to not recollect exactly what happened and the club has a policy of not being responsible for what happens to its members. The families have, of course, shown concern, but the police have not investigated this due to the background of those who have vanished. They are around the ages of 19 to 23 and tend to be rebellious go-getters or the extremely quiet types." He wiggled his eyebrows goofily.

"In addition, your little Keebler—"

"Kesler! He's not an elf that bakes cookies!"

"You sure about that? Well, your little math wiz plotted this point on the known cases. It was 60 miles away from the last report."

"What is the next step in this objective?" I was not thrilled that my fake boss was getting informational calls from my Chief first, but I was assuming it was because he was able to get out of class more than I. This caused another question to arise. "I assume Chief wants me to depart to investigate the situation after school today? I will contact her about getting clearance to get a W.A.V. to be on standby . . ."

"*We* leave for *our* mission at noon, my little kitty cat."

My jaw began to throb with the urge to cartoonishly drop to the floor. The fact that he was acting like he had this all figured out, the nerve of him including himself in my mission . . . until I realized the truth. How I wish it was fiction.

"But . . . I have to teach all afternoon . . ." I felt like a fish out of water, flopping for any and all excuses, but they sounded half-baked due to me not being able to catch my breath.

Mr. Jimmy Johns slid his fingers through his overly gelled hair, trying to look all suave. The calm gaze he cast down at me made me feel like a cold worm was wiggling down my spine. "I already informed the board office that I needed you to attend a meeting with me as a school rep for our backpack program."

I arched my eyebrow, my voice trying to quake, "What . . . will I tell my students? Who did you get to come sub for me??"

"Ms. Jessica, your preferred sub, who your kiddies adore. You also have the reputation of having the most detailed lesson plans in the building, so no issues with your curriculum being taught."

A single bead of sweat trickled down my neck, all of this happening too fast and becoming too real. I mean, actually working with General Jockstrap was too horrid to even conceive a thought about. "Well tough guy, what about you? Our new principal mysteriously leaving in the middle of the day. Do you want our school to fall apart?"

"Oh please! The principal could be gone for a week and the school would still be here. However, without our custodians, secretaries, and lunch staff, the building would be destroyed by the afternoon." I couldn't argue with that because I preached the exact same thing often to my fellow educators. Jeremey looked smug and satisfied as he leaned on the window to lock eyes on me. "Any other reason we can't depart in The Bringer Charger in twenty-two minutes, my sugar cube and honey biscuit?"

My brain was on the floor under me in a puddle, but I nodded by muscle memory, feeling so disconnected. He touched my shoulder in a half-hearted tender pat, the sensation causing me to jump a smidgen. "I will meet you across the street at the historical W.L. John's Center in eighteen minutes. I trust you to grab everything you need to prep for the assignment. I await our departure with eager fondness, dear lady." With these final directions, he bowed from his waist, spun once Michael Jackson style, and clicked his too expensive shoes together before walking off.

I had to hold my pulsing head while I walked down the hall as I tried to get back into combat mode, but it seemed to take its time, like it was trying to swim in an Olympic pool of melted peanut butter. Once I got to my classroom's hall with its lack of much sunlight, my thoughts sharpened and I cursed a slew of Japanese profanities as I got my Hunter supplies I kept in a Hello Kitty duffle bag (FYI: I did this before Ryan Reynolds' Deadpool made it the chimichanga coolest).

Right on the dot, I arrived at the W.L. John's Center. The Dare-to-be-Stupid King was about five feet from me, leaning on a column, a large visor style of glasses framing his face as he looked skyward. I glanced around the tranquil street, trying to sight one of our carrier vehicles, the odd sensation of waiting for my dad to pick me up in middle school hitting me. Then, my brain rolled back into gear, recalling something Jeremey said.

As if he was probing my mind (I pray that was all he was trying to probe if he wanted to keep all his knuckles), McShades lowered his no doubt designer sunglasses to attempt to give me that oh-so-sexy peek over. "The Charger is more than a set of wheels . . ."

The gale of wind that whipped up my hair in a personal tornado finished Jeremey's dramatic reveal. Regrettably, I gawked towards the sky like a massive idiot, a giant metal bird descending, its slick bleach white design contrasting to the elegant historical area we were in.

"Welcome to The Charger!" Jeremey shouted over the roar of the wind as he hopped with hip ease onto the low hanging ladder of the helicopter. The blades spun like a top out of control, making me dizzy. Heights still were not my friend after all these assignments; we were more like tolerable, forced acquaintances. Plus, being in a Bringer transport felt sickening despite its squeaky clean appearance. Unfortunately, I got the page from Chief about this assignment when I was packing my bag, it confirming everything The Phony King had said.

"Come, my darling! We have an adventure to begin!"

I stepped on the ladder reluctantly, merely to dodge his hand that he was attempting to pull me up with. *Ew.* No thank you to that physical contact. He jumped out of my way and bounded up and down like one of our kindergarten students, showing off everything as he informed the pilot, Brother Joe, it was time to take to the clouds. The pilot told me we were heading to Springfield and it would only take us two hours.

I still crave to hear the roar of the engine of my Kawasaki Ninja!

With this, I sat on the left side, away from the window and the giant pest with blond quills coming out of his finely groomed head. My time to focus was now as I reread the case reports and notes Kesler had documented and brushed up on some *lamia* lore Chief sent me. I was in my element, the zone of justice, the mode to destroy evil and protect those who could not protect themselves, a determination sang in my body and echoed into my soul. I would not lose, even if I had to stay cooped up with this *baka* for a few hours.

My resolve is stronger than that.

CHAPTER 7

I was almost wishing the helicopter would crash due to being tackled by a herd of flying elephants in tutus! That is how utterly annoying Super Trooper Gellaton was! Señor Jiminy Cricket in a course of two hours had a rock concert to Hannah Montana's season three soundtrack with a sparkly purple microphone that he for some dumb reason had attached on this chopper. When he wasn't shaking his ass like a baboon in mating season, he recited lines from King Lear in a nasally voice, loudly played 21 with some Playboy Bunny cards, and inhaled a whole Cornish game hen with savory vigor and delight.

I have never been so desperate to get out of a place in my life. I was on the verge of slicing his feet off with a butcher knife and jumping out of the helicopter before it even started descending. The only thing that saved me was my literal death grip on my armrest (I actually made a good-sized dent in it) and my K-Pop playlist blaring in my ears.

Once we hit solid ground and got the approval from the pilot, I nearly leapt off The Charger like my blood got zapped. Dare-to-be-annoying waved him off with an idiot movie star grin and a swagger that made his hips pop with too much sass. "*Ciao*, my friend!"

I think my chicken pita is going to come back up! Ah . . .

"All right now, the nectar to my flower! I hope you will give The Bringer's transport lines a good review on Yelp. There's a free air freshener in it for you." His arm was casually draped over my shoulder while his other was carrying his suit jacket over his shoulder like a lame cologne advertisement. "Although nothing smells as delectable as you, lovely princess—*Yelp!*"

I pinched his hand off me with such strength that he jerked away and dropped his jacket on the pavement. "There's your Yelp review. Now, please recall that we have an assignment to prep for before you give me another reason to rip your fingers one-by-one from your hand."

"You're so chilly, my pet." He dusted off his jacket, but seemed unfazed by my comment. "Our destination is about 1.3 miles from here. The club doesn't open until 6:00, but the employees will get there by 4:00 to prep for the evening."

"We need to find a place to change and equip our materials." I took a step forward towards the street, but was stopped by a voice in the wind behind me.

"I assume that includes weapons. How vulgar."

"Hm, we need to take all safety precautions in case the *lamia* tries to take any more victims tonight. My weapons are small, easy to conceal in regular standard issue gear, and can all harm a *lamia* if need be, or at least protect the club goers. That is our goal in case the investigation gets out of hand." I stared at him straight on, not ashamed of my ideals. I refused to have any more humans captured by a *monstrum* if I was there to stop them.

"Let's just blend in. I think that is the best method for getting our information. And above all, we will have fun. I can't wait to spin you on the dance floor!" Jeremey the Germy licked his lips in my direction before side stepping to the rhythm of the song he was humming, on his way to hail a cab.

"Dream on, Prince of the Pervs." And with that closing statement, I followed this fool on the hunt for a true monster.

* * *

The club, *Baile Oscuro*, was easy enough to find. The building shone like a dull obsidian, its slanted three story metal roof giving it an edgy feel. It was hard to tell in the back light of the sun if the building itself was fairly new or in its fifties. The bold neon sign had slashing lines in blue and lime green, steampunk gears made of massive, beaten tires that had red rims like flames engulfing the center. The name of the club was in a chilling print, but it had a forest green pepper with a dark purple rose on top of it at the end of *Oscuro*. The blend of Mexican and goth was apparent in the style. I knew this was going to be a unique experience.

As I jotted down notes of the exterior surroundings, mentally preparing myself to investigate the shrouded showered in darkness alleyway to the left, I got a glimpse of myself in the reflection of a bus stop across the street where I was at. It was a great effort not to groan and stomp. In my duffle bag, there are an array of clothes to blend in with the masses if need be compressed in vacuum-sealed bags. Chief tagged which one I had to wear and I was not gung-ho about it.

Darington was going to have a cow from delight. I'll probably have to pepper spray him on assignment and I am playing the self-defense ploy. That ripping his fingers off idea isn't off the table either.

My Hunters phone vibrated with a message and I had to push down the urge to groan once more. I could feel my eyebrow twitch with annoyance as I read:

All dressed for our rendezvous at this young folks club. I promise you will have to rip them off once the kiddies are away ‘꒰ It appears that the girls enter from the front of the building where the main neon sign is facing and the boys the rear. This allows them to do grand entrances with strobe lights for each member, giving them the goth Cinderella treatment. Never fear, my dear; I will only search and fall for you. You are the light in my lonely sea, my mermaid princess- 🖤

After I near regurgitated and wished I could claw my eyes out due to overly sickening emoji exposure, I about slipped on the pavement due to the shock that he quoted my favorite character from one of my all-time favorite animes. If he is stalking me, I swear his nuts will be crushed by my foot. Damn forced to share contact info with everyone in our organization! Good thing we destroy all our phones after a mission and get new ones with fresh numbers so we can't be tracked by the public.

The message continued:

> Like we discussed in the cab, I will be a ninja stealthing the areas closed to the public as you check the alleyway. I hate to think of you alone in a dark, secluded place without me to comfort you, but I will make up for it tonight 😘😘😘😘😘😘😘😘😘😘. I will tip Brother Bill well so he does not speak of the passion we will share after we have our first of MANY joint assignments! Let's take a selfie to document it later 😬 Meet you on the dance floor at admission hours. 😚 Miss you, my Venus.

A cracking sound stopped me from totally destroying my phone. I forgot to control my strength. My combat specialist would be proud. The *Power Rangers* theme song buzzed in my hand, my alarm warning me to start my task ringing. I got one more pouting glance at my reflection before I got into Hunter mode: "Whelp, looks like it's freakin morphin' time."

* * *

"So, you're a *Panic at the Disco* fan too?" This explanation came from the girl with a large purple lily embedded in a complex twist in her heavily dyed jet-hued hair. She was referring to one of the array of buttons that was strapped to my black moon cat purse: 'I Write Sins, Not Tragedies.'

"You know it! 'Victorious' is so my national anthem." I turned to inform her. I got a smooth, confident smile and a fist bump in return.

"Don't think I've seen you here before. First timer? Name's Lilly by the way, hence the hair accessory and I so love the outfit!" Lilly motioned elegantly with her eggplant-colored fingernails to my ensemble. A blush crept in my cheeks, my self-confidence shuffling in my stomach while the line inched forward a hair.

"Ahhh . . . I don't normally wear things like this. A friend recommended this club to me; I'm a fan of unique places. And my name is Anita." This was one of my aliases I used from work. Anita Mann. Say it slow, and you'll get it. Mr. Rick in our Human Relations Department has an odd sense of humor.

The pavement began to pulse in time with the booming bass that was coming out of the club. A burly, well-toned gentleman in a pure black matador suit with swirling tattoos on his beefy hands and hipster shades stood as the bouncer, checking IDs and stamping payers for admission. I had gotten in line after about a dozen girls were lined up, me not wanting to be too eager and to hide within society. Observing the patrons here and how they acted gave me a good indicator of how I should behave as well. Lilly ended up right behind me and had been a fun distraction until I gained access inside.

I hadn't heard anything from the Hamburgler yet. I tossed my phone into my purse, fake adjusting the strap to make sure my extendable gun was in my bust. The black corset style halter top helped keep all my weapons and assets in place, the matching flowing skirt concealing my Hunter utility belt under it. I was forced to wear a leather garter that had extra ammo and sprays in it. Looking at me straight on, all you would see is a girl in her mid-twenties in a corset halter dress from Hot Topic with a large studded diamond belt and a *sakura* blossom in her hair to add some color. Pretty average among all the pitch-toned outfits, heavy make-up, and bling.

My ears were thudding by the time I got my once-over and glow-in-the-dark hand stamp from the bouncer. Walking into the club, a scene of Hollywood fantasy hit me like a wave. The club itself was set up like most I've seen in films: metal stairs leading to a massive dance floor. Flashing lights illuminated the room, fog grooving on the floor with the several dancers swaying, and bubbles floating in the air like the whispers of friends. An overly populated bar had a long counter with colored lights embedded in it and one long mirror wall so people could see the flashy bartenders do flips with glasses and add a show to the liquid mixing. The DJ was appareled in a bold outfit with a mini matador hat and a ripped grudge shirt and jeans, getting into every beat with the music like the club goers. Music swelled in the air, the rocking pep of the Mexican notes' flare blending oddly with edginess of the punk sound. It really was a unique, but exciting place.

My first thought though after I took it all in was if they had tacos?

"Welcome to the *Baile Oscuro*, my fellow flower friend!" An arm was wrapped around me, a gentle hug from behind. I turned, slightly surprised, to see Lilly was the one who gave me the official introduction. "Sorry if I surprised you. You looked a little lost; don't need to scare a lamb off before she has had time to frolic in this special pasture."

A reassuring chuckle escaped my lips as I patted her hand once. "I'm good. Just taking it all in. It really does look smashing."

"Ha, ha! I love that! Smashing? You are so Brit-hip!" This made a real laugh come out. I was surprised how nice it was to spend time with a fellow female to simply have fun. That time in my life was over sadly. Still, Lilly was a precious person. I wanted to protect her, making the fire to stop this *lamia* burn hotter in my stomach.

"Are you meeting anyone here? You mentioned a friend." Her violet with red swirls contacts sparkled with curiosity.

I hadn't realized I was scanning for Jeremey so openly. The place was filling up with people, boys from the opposite set of stairs tracking down to hook up with ladies. I ducked my head, pretending to be interested in the DJ stand. "No, not overly."

"Well girl, you are too lovely to be isolated. Want to hit the bar?" Lilly looped her arm through mine so we could move out of the way from the tidal wave of people roaring in behind us. The bar was in sight, foam pouring from a mini fountain on the side of the counter.

"No thanks. I'm not really a drinker. I think I'll check out the dance floor."

"That sounds like a plan. I think I'm gonna get a Toxic Manzana and then I will see what sort of moves you got." She gave me a wink and then elbowed her way to get the attention of one of the cute bartenders.

She was a good girl. I swiveled and pivoted around the clusters of ladies swaying to a fast merengue song, boys mingling and flirting. The winks from the jewelry caught in the rainbow of lights, adding charm to the vibe of the room. This made it easier for me to focus as I examined the upper floor that I could see. There was a 'balcony' that overlooked the dance floor. In reality, it was only a thin single pole of metal that would barely block someone from leaning and falling to break their neck. When I craned my neck a bit more, trying not to fall on my rear, I could see the silhouettes of some door frames cast against the curtain of darkness in the background. The creepy way the darkness angled, it would be easy for someone, or something, to hide . . .

"Bailando" blurred from the speakers and the DJ spun on his table, lights and energy filling the room. The crowd shouted loudly in delight, powerfists punching in the air. Once the first verse started, the crowd scattered from their pairings and were segregated: girls on the left and boys on the right, to match the stairways they descended down. I stood there dazed and fully frozen in confusion. Flashbacks of middle school gym class dodgeball were filing into my mind.

"It's the single mingle jam." I jolted to the voice behind me, staring into the bright eyes of Lilly, a hand on her hip and drink in the other. Her cherry glittery lips held a smirk of whimsy as three other girls gathered around us.

"Okay . . . That doesn't help me much." I yelled over the deafening bass, leaning forward like a club noob. Which, ha, I was.

"At 7:00 on the dot until 7:20, the ladies come over here and then the men stay on their side and boogie together, scanning out on the other side who they would like to dance with. The DJ will wave his hand at 7:20 and then you are supposed to find a hottie from the other side to grind and groove against." The girls around us began gabbing and giggling

91

animatedly in Spanish, tapping my arm to get me into swinging my hips saucily like them.

"Mhmm ..." I expressed. Wasn't in love with this idea.

"Girl, let's get down!"

Lilly placed her drink on a tall table behind us and grabbed my arm, swaying me to the swell of the guitar. Luckily there was no mirror near me because I am sure my face would have shown me to appear like a frightened puppy. Lilly shouted words of encouragement and threw smiles at me as she began to dance gracefully in time with the tunes, her turns and hand motions making her look like a worthy empress of the night world. I barely moved my hands in the confines of my personal bubble, praying someone would not witness my seizure-like movements.

At the end of the song, the DJ seamlessly rolled into the next one, cheering on the boys filing in to join the waltz of bodies. To give them the star treatment, he shone the massive neon spotlight on the dude's side staircase. It seemed like, from that moment, my fairy godmother had a warped sense of humor.

At the top of the stairs, soaking in the scene in the room, was him. Jerk ... Dork ... Well ...

Wow. Looking at him, I couldn't come up with a rude remark. My movements stopped and once again, time seemed to float past me slowly, the background fading away as a force pulled my sight to only him.

To Jeremey.

He stood there in a pair of form-fitting, dark washed jeans and black and white checkered lace-up boots. A silk vest that caught designs in the light covered his chest while a black leather jacket with a pop of red peeking out around the lining concealed half of his arms. His shades were clipped on the side of a diamond studded belt. This being in front of me had the same flare for expensive and elegant fashion as the annoyance of a partner I have to work with, but there was an edge, an appeal, that made him blend into the assignment. At the same time, according to the swoons of all the ladies in the room, he stood-out.

What a messed-up Cinderella fairy tale I was in.

Like a prince of the goths, he descended slowly down the stairs, smiling tenderly at those he passed. In the middle of his journey, he paused and our eyes met. A light of recognition twinkled in the waves of his seaglass irises and a bright smile to match soon followed. A laser focus then followed as he made his way towards me. My chest began to hurt, my breathing ragged the closer he got. Once his shoes hit the floor, time restarted and he was bombard with guys trying to fistbump or introduce themselves.

And I was there, standing there, thanking the Lord he didn't get closer to me. The thought of it made me get goosebumps and my face feel flushed.

"AH!" I tripped forward slightly, barely able to catch myself. Behind me, Lilly chuckled and I could see from the thrust pose of her hip that she just booty-bumped me. "Sorry Anita! Trying to get you back in the swing. You sort of lost your cool when that hunk came down the stairs."

I brushed my skirt off so no one could see my face. It was still a tad hard to catch my breath. "I . . . I was . . . not . . . staring . . ." The words fumbled out. Why were they fumbling out?!

"Hey, girl? You were practically drooling . . ." She crossed her arms, giving me a wise look.

"BA! I WAS NOT!" The shout that exploded out of me was childish and sounded defensive. Lilly simply raised her eyebrow and the side of her lip followed suit, her facial expression telling me that she thought I was full of crap.

"That's bullshit, but whatever you want, Princess Peach! Let's get our lady friction on!" The gaggle of cute girls behind us gently pushed me into a dance circle.

Before I knew it, my hands were in the air, holding them to the beat of the music with these dance sisters I had magically acquired. We swayed, we chatted, we laughed. My energy recharged me, my chest feeling lighter and freer. This sensation of having a good time, being myself, no matter how uncoordinated I was, was a feeling I thought I had lost, one I was no longer accustomed to. And, it felt right.

"Kiss the moon goodbye, but don't close your eyes."

Selena Gomez played through the club, the liveliness of the song seeping into my veins. I was a fan of this song and my body reacted on its own to the opening verse, spinning and keeping time. Lilly was screaming about my great form, but it sounded like she was underwater, thousands of feet behind me. Perplexed, I opened my eyes to notice I was at the white line that separated the boys and girls. I wasn't sure how I got there, but that was my second question.

My first one was: why was I now forced to stare at Jeremey, a line the only thing keeping us apart? The confident, yet tender swagger of his dance moves had pulled me in once more. He had such graceful steps, smooth motions that made me feel dizzy. With our training, it was easy for me to see how he was a master in several self-defense arts for The Bringers. To others, he looked like a mean, lean goth-Mexican club scene dance machine.

His smile lifted when he saw me as my heartbeat fluttered into my throat. I think all the fog was messing with my brain. I hope there weren't any illegal substances in it. I was the poster child for D.A.R.E., so those experiences were beyond me. "Hey, beautiful," he mouthed, a gorgeous beam still plastered on his face.

This was all new to me: the atmosphere, sharing a mission, seeing him be more than a fake boss or a d-bag on a stage. My hand rose on its own, reaching timidly to give him a wave, butterflies slicing my stomach with this movement I caused. However, before my hand was too close, the DJ waved his hand boldly and the crowd roared, stampeding like in the *Lion King* to find the partner they were staring and longing after for an agonizingly long time.

I stepped back, fearful of what I was doing. I had a mission to complete, a *lamia* to track and kill; lives were on the line. Jeremey would follow me if he saw me run towards the second-story stairwell since he knew the layout. I didn't have to be here. I shouldn't be pretending I was a normal girl who was allowed a good time and a normal life. Retreating was the best.

I had only took two baby steps backwards when I bumped into one of the petite little Latina girls that I had been dancing by Lilly. Her smile at me was innocent and radiant, as she pointed to Jeremey across the way. *"Ve a estar con él."*

My Spanish was not the best, but it seemed like she was encouraging, or more like final cut scene before the boss, telling me that I needed to go to Jeremey.

I could feel my eyes widening in panic of worming my way out of this one, not wanting to disappoint this young lady who looked like she was spun out of magic and deep purple cotton candy. "Oh . . . Well . . . It's just . . ." GAH! My words were failing me. Why can't I deny it?

"Pssst, girl, get on with it! We all are dying to see you two hook-up!" The snort Lilly gave made me jump. Can't people just let me be?

I opened my mouth to decline, that I wasn't even remotely interested, but other words stole mine, "Would you care to dance now, my lady? I could not wait a second longer to get to know you."

A chorus of "awwwws" sang from the ladies behind me as a group had formed to stop and see the excitement. Never knew having a peanut gallery was so irritating. Loose hair was streaming down my face and I was desperately trying it to sweep it away as I answered, "Well, that is a very, umm, kind offer, but, I'm just not—"

Lilly came to my side and booty bumped me forward again. I went flying into Jeremey's open arms, his chest the only thing blocking me from a nasty faceplant. Before I could glare daggers at my flowered friend and give her a choice word or three, Jeremey grabbed my hand sweetly and led me to a more open area of the dance floor.

"So, here we are, my beautiful goddess. My Lord, you look so divine that I feel sinful touching you, but I'm ready to go to Hell for you." Jeremey's grin was solely for me as he leaned his face closer to mine so all I could see was him and the lights blinking in rhythm from above. Having him so near made me feel like I had been punched in the gut, but his comment made me want to gag. I knew how to respond to that.

"Ha, well, don't you know we're all going to Hell, Jeremey? And I know your compliment isn't sincere, so you can cut your bullshit." I looked away, trying to find an exit to formulate a plan, but McNugget Pants was not giving me much room to move from his embrace.

Without warning, he spun me into a flashy twirl that matched the crescendo of the music, making the witnesses who were gawking sigh and cheer outwardly. I fell into his chest again, taking three counts of breath to truly not vomit. Anger flared up in me, but the look on his face snuffed it out in an instant. The way the light bounced off his spikes, his face looked boyish and compassionate, and . . . slightly stung.

His grip on my hand got tighter and he hugged me full on, his hand sliding, trailing down my hips and the edge of my hair, as if teasing me into wondering if he was going to touch my butt or not. I shivered despite myself, electricity sizzling on my skin. I didn't like feeling bound by him, so I looked up to see if his look had changed. It hadn't.

"Val . . . you truly look gorgeous tonight. Seeing you like this, in fun, pretty clothes and having a good time . . . it makes me happier than I thought. It makes me want to be with you more, really be with you and protect you. Let me . . . let me stay here like this for a while." With his comment, he wrapped his arms even tighter around me, my whole body pressed so close to his that I could feel my portable gun digging deep into my cleavage.

I squirmed to look at him once more, the red and blue hued lights making my vision blurred and my face feel too warm. "Are you on drugs Darington or are you just damn crazy?"

He threw his head back and laughed at that. "I'm intoxicated by the woman that is you and mad with love. Is that the answer you wanted, my missing piece?"

I bit my lip away from him, focusing on the floor. This man was making me tired, but at least I knew how to handle him like this. "You're an asshat." I rested my arm on his tricep, which I sadly had to admit was impressive. "What did you find out about upstairs?"

He shook his head as if to scold me and then nodded. "Always down to business. How cold, my ladybug. But, to answer you, the upstairs is made up of rooms that seem to be storage rooms and a few offices. They are beat to all hell and from the paint chips, I'd say this place was new in the 50s. My guess is it was a theater since the thin railing up there reminds me of where stagehands would work lights and they have those massive black curtains on both side."

Ah. Now that made sense. I noticed how abnormally dark it was up there. The curtain of darkness I saw was, literally, curtains! "Their lighting system up there must suck."

"Yeah. The main hall's is broken. I couldn't find a working switch anywhere. However, it seems the three ajared doors have lamps in them that give off the eerie glow of light they have. The floor is not very sturdy either and made a lot of noise."

I graced him with a tiny smile of relief. "Lucky you weren't caught."

"I know, right?!" He exclaimed joyfully. He turned me around once more and we moved our hips in time together. I was adjusting to his steps, his body heat, the essence of him without realizing it. I blinked hard, keeping our conversation on track.

"Is there a third floor?"

"Yes and no. It seems like it's a ventilation system up there, with maybe part of a roof up behind the large neon sign. I found some ratty, old metal stairs, but all I heard were dusty fans buzzing, so I wasn't going to risk getting this lovely head chopped off for that. How was the left alleyway?"

"Pretty standard for dark, dirty, city alleyways. It's not nearly as cleaned-up as the right one where the boys enter for their back entrance. Other than a dull streetlamp in front of it, there's no light, making it a better place to have a drunken fight. But——" I nibbled on my lip as Jeremey grabbed me and whirled me in the air with a grace that left me feeling awed and cold. Once again, the peanut gallery swooned and applauded. The feeling of being weightless and addressed like a princess flattered me. My voice was sinking, trying to grasp the reality of how to continue.

"Sorry for interrupting you. Please continue." His cheesy grin looked bemused as he nudged me to keep talking.

"I . . . well, umm . . . The . . . the alleyway I investigated leads straight to another open street with old time shops, but it's easy to see off into the horizon a field of tall wheat. I heard water, but I couldn't overly see much past the wheat except some skinny trees way-off in the distance. With all this darkness and that open field, I feel like—"

"This is a good place to capture targets . . ." Jeremey finished. An eerie silence engulfed us, my ears ringing with the pressure of how haunting this all was.

"We need to report to Chief what we found. Maybe we can get a move on with them setting up some trained under-cover bouncers from our groups. We need to—"

Jeremey cradled me against him yet again, leaning near my ear. His breath was warm and tickled my skin, my neck getting prickles of delight. The intoxicating scent of sandalwood hit me, causing me to spin. My head pounded in time with the music and my heart thudded, yearning for something I didn't understand, my stomach becoming queasy.

"Stay with me a moment longer, Val. I don't want this to end. This dance. This night. This contentment. I just want you to understand me." I could feel his eyes burning a hole in the top of my head.

"Jeremey, we have to do our mission, but, I . . . I will tell you . . ." My chest was jackhammering, my face flushed with heat. I cannot believe I am going to tell him this, but in the spell of this melody, of this evening, I felt compelled to, like he needed to hear it. "You . . . you look . . . you look very handsome in those clothes tonight. They . . . they look dashing . . . on you . . . Jeremey . . ."

I wanted to learn to dig and burrow myself into a tunnel to go to China. My face was as beat red as a cherry from the reflection I could see in a stream of bubbles that passed us. I was ready to erase this from my memory, this lapse in judgement of me trying to be kind to a Bringer. When I finally jerked my head to look at Jeremey yet again and not past him, the stare I received back was one that was lost, resetting itself. I thought he had frozen in place, five long seconds of a techno-beat passing by us. However, he proved me wrong.

With a mighty leopard-like leap, he clung closer to me, nuzzling his nose against my neck, the static energy from his lips almost tangible on my flesh. It took all my willpower not to exhale or succumb to the stirrings in my chest. Emotions were unwinding so fast within me that I could almost see them as colors before my eyes: I wanted to punch, scream, hit, wail, flee, but I also wanted to stay, embrace, accept, find tenderness, return . . .

Jeremey didn't give me much time to try to sort out the tangled weave I had become. His lips finally made contact with the edge of my ear, a gasp escaping before I could smash it. My mouth opened to protest, but only hard air came out. I could feel his lips forming a smile behind my earlobe, followed by a playful bite actually on my lobe. I had to chomp down on my lip to not cry out, moisture building in my eyes.

Damn him. Damn him for toying with me, acting like he cared for me, too many normal humans around to deck him to Hawaii like I wanted to. Damn him for making me freeze up, become stone, him being the only person in ages to do this to me. Damn him for confusing me, making my head spin, my body react, deep down wanting him to explore more of me. Damn him for having to work with me. Damn me for being a scaredy cat. Damn him! Damn him! DAMN HIM!

One of his supporting hands held the back of my head, stroking my hair with affection that made me on edge and relaxed at the same time. His lips travelled up my ear in slow increments until he got to the middle, his tongue deciding to take a turn. Jeremey licked the inside of my ear, sending my nerves into a panic attack and making my feet glue to the floor.

Of course he had to do that, I thought snarkily to myself. *I wish my stupid voice would work like God intended so I could fucking tell him off!*

"Hey . . ." I was finally able to force out after about fifty-seven devastating failures. "Look . . . Jer—" I had to stop, a finger going down my back as he trailed down my neck with sweet pecks. It was getting hard to breathe, but I barreled forward, "Hey. Listen, we really need—"

An aroma of rotting flesh hit my nose, making me stiffen up on instinct. Jeremey noticed it as well, his arms dropping to my hips, barely pressing them, as if he was preparing to protect me. My blood crackled with adrenaline, my instincts speeding into overdrive. Jeremey and I both kept our stances still, but our eyes were scanning every nook and cranny, each face in the crowd for any sign of the supernatural. The scent had not returned. Maybe it was just my imagination, but from the hair on my arms standing up on their own, that couldn't be.

A scraping sound surfaced, making both our necks snap upward to the railing. It was very quiet, but the noise was so sickeningly ... unnatural. "Something's upstairs?" My voice was hallowed, a wisp of a whisper.

The spikes on Jeremey's head swayed forward as he nodded. "After you, my dear."

With this, my vision caught a flash of a shadow dashing across the balcony above the main part of the dancefloor. It appeared to be the trick of the eyes, unless you knew what to look for.

With that, I bolted out of Jeremey's arms with ease, sprinting and curving around dancers who were getting their fast-tempo groove on. I backtracked up to the stairs I first entered up with Lilly, not caring if my forced on me companion was following. Sliding towards the bathrooms, I raced up the stairs as efficiently and silently as my boots could take me, going two at a time.

The second floor was just as Jeremey described. The limited light closed in on me, but I tackled past it, having to halt to a stop past the center of the ancient hall. And that's when the blink of darkness I saw zoomed behind me once more. It was so speedy that I could hardly process it. I had almost literally slammed on my brakes to stop my movement, but I stumbled slightly and the baby wedge I had on my boots cracked, making me jerk forward.

"Tee-hee-hee ..."

A bone-chilling chuckle echoed around the upper perimeter, turning my blood into ice. My feet rooted into the ground, as if the sound effect had glued them into place. However, I reacted quickly and grabbed my gun, pointing it and my taser from my under skirt belt in one swift motion. I was prepared for whatever was coming my way.

The aura around me began to get thick, like a bubble pocket had engulfed me and the presence that was glaring me down, the blob of darkness. "*Lamia* . . ." I huffed out heatedly, seeing if this would cause a reaction. I got my answer.

"Ah, HEE-HEE! Welcome to our web, little mouse."

This voice was two trying to make a harmony, but it clashed, the words tripping all over each other to be heard. Pitches climbed up the walls, making my face prickle. One tone was a normal male voice, but the other was an abnormally sinister, highly-pitched bass, a sound that shouldn't be possible. It was like this person was speaking into a voice box with extreme auto tune, but it was embedded too deep into its throat. The laugh was too perfect for a psycho villain from a movie.

An overhead light began to swing in a creaking motion, one that acted like a bolt had weaseled its way off the hinges. The echoing from the metal sound blending with the continued laughter made my nerves throb like mad. My back hunched up on its own, causing me to swivel my body to aim my gun at the presence behind me. My weapon extended forward in a thrust, it making contact with a slightly tangible form. Before I could release my trigger, it zoomed away from me and I had to grab my gun with my other hand to stop the motion of shooting.

Was that the *lamia* or this creepy laugh I had been hearing? Were they one in the same? No . . . This presence in the room with me was of another being, but the energy entombing me was a powerful psychic entity. I may actually be trapped in this bubble, the pull around it pulsing loudly in my ears. My vision began to get clouded, but my mind was sharp, calculating angles in the ceiling to see if I could track this opponent better. The muscles in my legs were buckling from being forced to remain in one position, one stance. No matter how much strength I used to move my feet, it was wasted efforts.

"Tee-hee . . . you seem stuck there, little girl."

A shiver went up my spine, so I repaid the favor by elbowing hard the figure I could sense behind me. The motion made contact with something, a grunt echoing through the rafters. This gave me the surprise advantage on the *monstrum* in the room, getting me unstuck. I charged forward in the direction of the grunt, smacking into a solid form. The form went flying upward, banging against the metal with a thud that was barely canceled out by the ironic timing of an edgy crescendo of a song. However, the being didn't fall down, but more floated in place. My first thought was a rope had snagged him from behind, but the confident cat-who-swallowed-the-canary grin shone in the backdrop of darkness that blanketed us proved I was wrong.

The mass I hit was not a *lamia*. Its structure was too solid. *Lamia* are rail-thin and bony. The collision I had proved to me I had encountered a creature close to Jeremey's build, but less firm from intense workout.

"That wasn't very nice. You don't like that . . . do you?" The creepy phantom voiced, extending his arms as if he was a martyr nailed to a cross.

Fog rose around me, ensnaring me by my waist, squeezing my stomach hard. I fought against the wave of nauseousness from the pressure, ready to pounce on the figure mocking me whipping out my now activated taser. But, instead of landing a hit, I was thrown into the air and received a blow from an invisible hand. My wheels were spinning, my hearing dying in and out, but just enough of my sanity was intact to get a bone-chilling hum to enter my ears from the right.

I elbowed past the scrapes on my arms as speedily as I could manage to knock out this villain I could see. The sinister nasal cackling continued as the being floating in the shadows swung to the beat with his howling, his arms still outstretched scarecrow style. Being shoved by an invisible hand, the creature swung back and forth in a violent motion. I dodged the first three attempts of him trying to tackle me, but he gained velocity and I got whacked hard in the chin, my knees giving out from under me and my taser sliding across the floor with a clack.

As I slowly lifted my forehead off the metal ground, I could feel it was wet, blood dripping down the bridge of my nose. Carefully, I was able to get to my knees, lights of dull colors blinking in front of my eyes. The confines of this space and with so many mortals below had made me too cautious. I spat on the floor towards my attacker, showing my disgust as I prepped my gun next to my hip.

"Ha. You're an annoying bastard, aren't you?" A raspy tone I didn't like came out of my mouth.

The swinging figure lurched forward, acting like he was going to grab me, but his motion barely missed. I had a feeling he was toying with me, that whatever help he had with this twisted flying act could have taken me out easily in my ragged state.

"We will knock you down like your precious groups destroy the *monstrum*, creatures you fear, beings far more superior than yourself. That is why you lash, with your weapons and resourcefulness. Your fear. Tee-hee. You think you're *better* than them, yet you are *afraid* of them. Tee-hee. Why are you so determined to not let them be, so foolish as to not work with them? They should take out the weak, the evil, the useless. Let them feast on those humans you judge, your own kind you dub unworthy, and the world will benefit. Let the *monstrum* guide you."

The large figure cocked his head with a snap, a crack that sounded unnatural and made his head appear to be detached as it drooped too low on his left side. Yet, his cruel beam continued to speak, shining through the darkness straight into my soul. It was so messed up that I yearned for it to be pitch black for once.

"You need to accept your fate, you special little mouse. Or succumb to become a lush substance for Master; he enjoys draining the force out of pretty maidens... Tee-hee... Tee-hee... HAHAHAHAHAHA!" The heavily vibrating, autotuned voice kept changing frequencies, making my legs rubbery and head feel like it was going to split in two. Once it went into a fit of uncontrollable, Satanist cackling, I had had enough.

The roar of its howling was unbearably loud, echoing against the metal around us. I felt surrounded by iron bars while it was raining glass shards all around me. There was no way we could hide this from the mortals now. I'd have to take my case and then pull this freak into the shadows before my cover was blown.

While he kept his laughing going, near choking on his own air supply and bile, I shouted so I could be heard, "Fucking shut your trap!" And stood to three-quarters' height to take a shot, the blast of the gun tearing through the ripples of sound. The small light of the bullet being shot out blinded me for a second. I wasn't sure if I hit my mark, but the blob that was on a soapbox high was no longer in front of me.

I pushed the button on my Hunters' signal that was attached to my underbelt to let them know we had a high level encounter and we would need an agent and team for either back-up or cover. I sadly would need some medical attention as well before I debriefed to Chief. A checklist of procedures was going through my mind on autopilot as I stumbled forward to assess the damage, half expecting a horde of bouncers and police to charge up the stairs.

"Your mind is strong there, young maid. That will make you taste all the sweeter as I dry you into a wrinkled husk of nothingness." A new voice entered the fray that I thought was over. Unlike the last one, it was light, airy, aristocratic, a standard elegant voice that made one's bones chill on impact and face flush with wonder. It was from a fantasy and almost registered in a different airwave than a human one. There was no doubt this was a divine characterized voice.

This was the *lamia*.

I knew he was with me, maybe right beside me, but I could not see him at all. He blended perfectly into the darkness as if he was one with it, fused to him like another skin. Perhaps, with his abilities, he was. My arms were suddenly force-tied behind me with a jerk and I was plopped roughly onto the floor like a rag doll. The wind was knocked out of me and all I could see were speckles of gray winking from the floor design my face was being rubbed into. A force was pushing me down, laying on top of me. I tried to kick my legs so I could shatter the shield I was smashed under in some way, but they felt like putty. My hands were tied against my back with ropes I knew didn't truly exist, but I felt digging into and burning my flesh.

"Screw . . . you! I'm . . . a . . . Hunter. You are a murderer, regardless . . . of your species . . . That makes . . . you scum. Don't make some . . . minion . . . speak for you . . . like a puppet. That just . . . shows . . . weakness . . ." I struggled to breathe those words out, but my malice was hard in each word, so much so that I could feel the binds drowning me shrink into itself a bit.

I'm not going out like this! This is my vow I made to myself as I fought against the psychic weight.

I heard then the scraping of long fingernails on the railing to my right, a bolting pain in my eardrums. The *lamia* made a sound as if it was thinking about what I said. "You are rather unique and I adore your vigor, but I will not have a deformed bitch speak to me in that way. You are my sustenance, fair maid, and I cannot wait to touch every prickle on your flesh and lick each bead of sweat off your brow from your fear. How strong you will make me, this purpose more fitting for you. I will make it slow, so you can feel the lasting effect of my fingers on your body—"

CRACK!

The *lamia's* speech was interrupted by a hard smack in the middle of his face. Although I could barely turn my head, I saw through a haze that the blood sucker had been kneed in the face hard. For a split second, I saw his powdery white face with a large fracture going down from his forehead to his lips as though he was made of porcelain. He lurched backwards and then melted into the blackness that concealed the pitch hall, the energy he was using to pin me fading away.

"Don't lay a finger on my girl." As I clawed my fingers into the firm floor to give me some support and traction to get up on my knees, I was staring at the presence of Jeremey. He had a white leather jacket over his goth get-up and a smug look of satisfaction locked-on where the *lamia* had once been, his hands in his pocket all too casual. He was a lighthouse, a beacon of light, literally glowing in a yellowish tint and his spikes a dazzling white, near the shape of the rays of God in paintings. He was a comforting contrast to the darkness I had been battling in, but it was still sickening to look at him for too long.

I was able to get to my elbows and push up until Darington grabbed my hand and pulled me up, resting his hand on the small of my back for support. A smile was still plastered to his face, but his sea-green eyes were roiling with concern. "Val . . . are you all right?"

He bent down so I could wrap one of my battered arms around his neck as he went on, "I was taking data on the side, but it was near impossible to see anything! Once that Poptart started floating though, I couldn't get to you. It was like he vacuum sealed you in a bubble. I could feel you, but I couldn't see or hear you and I assume the same happened to you. I kept crying your name, but nothing. When I charged into it, it was like I phased through it and I ended up at the far end of the hall. I was getting desperate, so I used my best knee strikes until I suppose I popped the bubble enough to make an impact. I'm so glad I cracked his shitty face before he got to you. You're my girl to torment, and only I can touch your body and send thrills to it." He winked at the end of his recap, although his eyes were misty with what seemed like legitimate worry.

"Yeah, I heard." I huffed outwardly, annoyed but with no real energy to roll my eyes like I wanted to. I was literally having to use him like a crutch until my legs could stop shaking like leaves on a tree. "Let me guess . . . Muay Thai?"

"You do know your martial arts, my bud in spring." His smile became wide and blinding.

A snort erupted out of me as I fought against the fog swirling in my brain, I grasping for my autopilot checklist for normalcy. My head leaned towards his chest, something catching my eye. "Your shirt is ripped down the middle..." I noticed three lines that looked like slash marks going down in a bold diagonal pattern about ten inches long each.

He shrugged and looked head-on, assessing the room. "Yeah, that stupid punk with the cringy cackle rammed into me and my shirt got caught good on the railing, slicing it. I had a supply backpack I hid up here during my investigation early and lucky once I got the bastard off me, I was on the same side as the bag to get my coat. I paged The Bringers, but I saw the blinking light through the mist of your pager too. We should have back-up real soon. Our goal right now is to get you out of here."

I nodded solemnly, allowing Jeremey to lead me out of a set of stairs that led to an exit just as I heard sirens in the distance. That was our call, a warning that things were worse than they first appeared.

CHAPTER 8

"This report is disturbing . . ." Mr. Stillman's calm voice seemed to bang through the small meeting room myself, Jeremey, Chief, and he were in. The lights in the overly crisp white space seemed to be draining him of his energy, the lines in his face more profound. His expression was saddened, making him age ten years in an instant, his clear eyes looking vivid.

"Indeed." Chief kept her composure, leaning slightly on the edge of the metal staff desk in the room's corner. She had her arms crossed and her expression thoughtful, but I saw some pinched up spots on her face. Her standard black pencil skirt and blazer set-off against the bleach-colored room, near commanding us to look to her for wisdom and strength. Chief Beryl Edric radiated guidance swift and true, like her Raven Clan heritage.

"We could hardly see anything, so they chose their location flawlessly." This came from Jeremey, who was sitting next to me in a hard metal chair. We both had our hands folded in our laps, nervous and still in a bit of shellshock from the intensity of this fight. My heart now ached for those men drafted at a young age forced to go to war, a conflict that they would never fully understand and how they were basically thrown into a grinder of pain and carnage. Jeremey and I seemed like fresh agents.

"As far as we can calculate, following the format of this *lamia*, they have taken at least ten victims that we know of. The club seems to be his only repeat supply bank of food, but after you two escaped, I am sure he has moved on." Chief stated, adjusting her glasses.

"You're sure this vampiric creature was a he?" Mr. Stillman asked inquisitively, his eyes looking innocent with grandfatherly worry.

Jeremey elbowed me lightly in the arm, making me start in my seat. I hadn't realized Mr. Stillman had been addressing me. It made sense since I was the only one who had truly heard his voice. I nodded in jerky motions, trying to hide my embarrassment. "Yes, it was that haunting tone and had an air of self-importance that doesn't sound like it fits in our world."

"And he was able to pin you down with some sort of... otherworldly energy?" Chief never liked to say the word psychic for the almost hocus-pocus definition that mortals have given it. I personally used psychic as my favorite type of *Pokemon*, but Chief didn't need that info. Still, it made me feel a smidgen lighter in my chest and I needed a bit of relief from the tight pressure building. And, honestly, psychic was the best word to use in this case. There was no other way to describe it.

"Yes, Chief." I nodded again, shame washing over my face. "I ... I wasn't expecting there to be two beings in the club and one that was clearly ..." I swallowed on a lump in my throat, the words a chore to get out, but I didn't want to share this in the report yet for all to see. I wanted to get the Chief's opinion first.

"Human ..."

A collective gasp came from both our bosses. Mr. Stillman crossed himself and his eyes became abnormally buggy, his face getting pastier with fear. Chief had the opposite effect, her eyes becoming steely and her face flushing with anger.

Jeremey stared at me in surprise, but in a blink, the expression was replaced with one of trust and acknowledgement. "I had suspected that, but he was so concealed in darkness and fog that it was hard to make-out its figure. And his voice ... it was heavily autotuned, mixing high-pitched sounds with bass. I thought my ears would bleed when it cackled. I can't imagine how Agent Hemmingway handled it being closer and all that."

"Yes, the fact she was trapped in a bubble of otherworldly energy is sickening and scary." Chief placed her fist under her chin, a motherly look coming across her face. "I'm sorry you had a rough time, Valda. I'm just glad you're safe now."

"It's fine Chief. Anything I could do to help with the investigation. I'm just glad no one was taken when we went over the records." The Hunters had sent a group of undercover investigators to check the attendance records (no matter how minimal they were) to see if anyone was missing and The Bringers called in the local police force, an anonymous caller complaining about a noisy commotion on the second floor. Anyone could guess this was Jeremey.

"The question at hand is why would a human be working with a vampire?" Mr. Stillman voiced the elephant in the room.

"The powers would perhaps be alluring to humans, who feel mundane in comparison." Chief hypothesized.

"Media about monsters in recent years doesn't help, giving illusions that monsters are misunderstood." Jeremey stated, a sentence that seemed to counter with The Bringer's mission.

"But, why this human? How did he encounter this powerful night creature?" Mr. Stillman questioned.

"Did the human, with what you could see Agent Hemmingway, seem to have special traits?" Chief tightened her ponytail, it looking immaculate.

I nibbled on my bottom lip slightly, trying to recollect through a mental haze what I truly could see through the actual fog of the previous night's battle. "The human couldn't have been much taller than me. It did have a bigger bone structure and a large, creepy smile." A thought rushed into my head and seemed to smack me in the forehead, a memory surfacing. "The eyes . . . they were clear, except for dull red swirls all inside the irises. It seemed like it was natural too, not contacts or a trick of the light."

"Possession?" Chief asked.

"Maybe. It felt like he was willingly being controlled." I rested a hand on my cheek, thinking hard to see if I could grasp for a better image to describe from my archives of memories, but all I was getting was a headache.

"And that voice . . . This human could have been speaking in his own voice and had the vampire's on top of it, hence the wild sounds that were hard to process." Jeremey hit his chin now with a fist as if trying to knock information into himself.

"What I do not understand is why a vampiric creature would want to work with a human, a being it sees merely as a meal." The quiet, cracking sound of Mr. Stillman's voice stopped our gears to a halt, all our attention being drawn to him.

"Money? An influential family?" Jeremey gave some suggestions.

Chief shook her head in deliberate motions, her movements so slow it looked as if she could hardly hold her head up anymore. "For a mortal, those would be good points to look for in an underling, but with the power of a *lamia* that can blend so effortlessly into the shadows, basically cannot be sensed, and has exceedingly powerful possession abilities, I see no logical need for this human to be of use to him."

"He must be trolling with us . . ." I muttered in a huff, feeling exhausted.

"Valda, don't joke about trolls." Chief wagged her finger at me.

"Yes ma'am."

Mr. Stillman gave me an attempt of a smile, his eyes regaining a bit of his luster in them, making the forest green and caramel brown of his sweater vest pop. "You two have been through a lot tonight. Thank you very much for your information and work on this assignment, Brother Jeremey and Ms. Hemmingway. Please, get some rest and we will be in touch soon."

He inclined his head to the clock to indicate it was two in the morning. I had to get looked over closely by our medical staff after we were given a change of clothes. Nothing was amiss with me luckily, but I will have to wear blazers and no low-neck shirts to work to cover my deep cuts and bruises. Jeremey, my 'principal,' wanted me to stay home to recover, but there's no rest for the wicked, as they say. Plus, I missed my classroom babies.

"I agree with Mr. Stillman. Thank you for staying to give us this data and a private, much-needed debriefing. We will get to work on tracking the next location and potential spots with our team quickly and give you any information you need once we know. Thank you for your work and safe travels home." Chief and I saluted each other and Mr. Stillman and Jeremey lightly embraced before we were led out by our night shift security team.

"Val . . . ?" Jeremey touched my shoulder, making me halt and flinch. He retracted it back and looked at me apologetically. "I'm sorry. Is it still tender?"

He was referring to when I had been dropped by the psychic whips of the *lamia*, but that was not why my body reacted. I still recalled all the words spoke, so sweet, the way his flesh felt on me, the hold he had on me that made me almost miss true, intimate contact. I pray that the *lamia* was using his abilities early to weaken me and this feeling of being a puddle of hormones was due to a supernatural dick creature.

Well, one other than Jeremey that is.

"No . . ." I dragged out. "I'm just tired."

"That's why you should get some rest. I can come in a bit later tomorrow, but you don't have that luxury. We can say you started feeling ill at the meeting—"

I placed my hand in front of his face to cease Jeremey from talking more. Okay! This calling him Jeremey crap needs to stop ASAP! "Like I'm that weak. You're just a dinosaur who needs his old man rest." I rolled my eyes towards him, a smug smile tugging at my lips.

Ham for Brains (Oh! That felt good) let out a hard laugh, raising an eyebrow at me. "Well, I can't force a beautiful and heavily trained woman against her will. Just . . . take care of yourself, Val." He gently stroked my cheek with the back of his hand, a current of affection washing over us from the look he replied to mine with his eyes. "I'll see you in the morning.

Let me know if you need anything." And with that, he turned around to head towards the parking garage, not another glance thrown my way.

I didn't like this compassionate side to Darington, this side that made him feel near humane and foreign to me. My face was becoming warm, like I had covered myself up with too many of my nerdy fleece blankets. But, I was too exhausted to really want to dig deeper into the conversation and moments I had at the club with Jeremey. Heck, I wanted to just destroy them forever, like shaking an Etch-a-Sketch hard. That's probably what his brain would sound like if I shook him good. I'll have to try that in the future, for science's sake.

Dragging myself to pass the cubicle area, I decided to get a Yoo-hoo for the road. I most likely wouldn't be allowed to drive this late after every-thing that happened, but I wanted to be semi-alert in case and it was way too late for coffee or soda. Don't need chest pain all night. Man! Tomorrow was going to be a long day . . .

Hearing the ping of my money getting eaten by the machine, I was prepared to press the button for my choice of beverage when at a messy work table, I saw a cluster of wild, fiery red hair and what looked like a teddy bear in a corduroy vest hunched beside the bush of red. I blinked to make sure I truly was seeing them and I was. Kesler and Bonnie were sitting there, together, close, looking over some files together. Smiles were glued on their faces as they made casual conversation between finding data. I felt bad they got called in so late to help us, but this is the nature of the beast (ha) with our job. Everyone here has to do it often, but it's not easy.

Still, after everything tonight, I was happy I got to witness this little moment. I lifted my Yoo-hoo can in the air with a tiny grin. "Here's to you, kids." and walked the opposite direction. I was pleased to see them at least smiling and comfortable with each other. I would have to tease, I mean, get the details, from Kesler in a day or so, since he'd be the first to call me once he found any patterns. Or, worse option, didn't.

"You spying on the fruitloop, girlie girl? Didn't your mother tell you it's not nice to eavesdrop?" I turned to come face-to-scar with Galen, his

113

looming figure covering me, but I brushed off his comment like it was nothing.

"Shining your pretties kinda early today, eh there Captain Glum?" I jested with him, a spark of my sarcasm starting to sink back into my soul. Yoo-hoo does a body good.

He gave me his stereotypical "hmph," his jaw squared tight before bantering back, "I normally get here around three in the morning to prep the weapons and do a warm-up work-out for myself before doing the early morning sessions. And if you must snark at my routine, I was here early sharpening some new wooden beauties and polishing swords, including your damned *katana*, so be grateful."

"Don't curse at my *katana*, old man! I got that from my *sensei* in Japan." My hair flew in my face as I glared up at him. I knew I was not truly upset with him, but no one jokes about my metal baby. But, my curiosity got the better of me. I'm worse than a *neko*. "So . . . what sort of new beauties did you get in?" I slanted my eyes coyly, puckering my lips in pretend indifference.

A smug look etched into his cheeks. "Some nice clubs made of super tough cedar from the Himalayas. A rare find, true cedar trees. Took some strong letters and calls to get them."

"Those will be good for those pesky brownies. Stupid, ankle-biting bastards! But, I suppose we got them to do some lethal damage on those nasty Pishacha that had been terrorizing the India unit. Damn *monstrum* are now taking our melting pot policy to heart." I was so done with flesh and body stealers.

"Hmm, as always, you are very well-informed, missy. Are you trying to get some rest now, slick?"

I sighed heavily, having to stifle a yawn that wanted to come out after. "Yeah, but now I'm debating if the long drive home would be worth it for only a few hours of sleep. Socks has enough food and water, but I'll miss her. Darington said I could call out sick to rest, but I don't roll like that." My eyes were burning from exhaustion, but my mind was dizzy from all the racing thoughts I was trying to snuff out. Sleep would be unlikely no matter where I was.

"Oh yeah. I heard about you being forced to work with a pansy Bringer, and it had to be Cracker Dick out of all of them. I wouldn't even wish that on you." We shared a rueful smile. Galen and I may go round-and-round at times, but we understood each other. Plus, we were both pretty kick-ass.

I felt a hard thump on the top of my head. I grunted outwardly in discomfort and irritation. Bet I'll have a goose egg now on top of all my other lovely marks. Delightful. "You're not gonna sleep, kid. Come on. Let's go get some black java. It'll make you grow a pair, something all you youngsters need."

I stuck my tongue out at his comment, but followed without making a peep. I was gonna drown my coffee in sugar and salted-caramel creamer and he can call me a fairy princess all day for it. Don't care. I'm a Hunter. I do what I want!

In the middle of our Hunter's Headquarters was a hub that consisted of several tall tables, a cafe and cafeteria that is always filled with goodies. Four large TVs were mounted around the crisp, open space. On the left corner, there was a large fish tank and a pool table. To the right, a lounging area of comfy couches and armchairs, several outlets and ports for easy access made it a good place to chill. A cart of 18 high tech laptops and IPads were there for check-out with the building. Lavender and warm vanilla filled the room, its effects calming and homey.

Galen and I got our beverages and found a corner seat by a luscious bamboo plant. The steam from my cup warmed the tips of my fingers, the fragrance seeping into my veins slowly. We sipped in a content silence for a few minutes, my eyes absorbing my surroundings, this ruly ordered place a beacon in a realm of chaos. This place was home, my safe harbor and I was grateful to it. Looking at it now, I had a loving sense to protect everything The Hunters stood for, a pride and loyalty swelling strong within me.

"So . . . you doing okay, kid? Seriously?" Galen dragged out, breaking my spell of solitude, my cone of silence.

"Psst. What's with the fatherly side of you?" I narrowed my eyes, a mocking smile playing on my lips.

"Shut your trap! I hate having them Bringers in our compound. I could blow this *lamia's* fucking head off if they'd let me." His gruff voice had some added some vigor in it. I could literally hear his testosterone levels rising from his tone.

"Ha. Well, I don't doubt your skills or how badass your explosions are, but this *lamia* . . . It was like nothing I had ever encountered. It wasn't hardly even tangible. I've dealt with things that are hard to see, can blend into the background, or even become invisible for a bit, but not one that can fuse with darkness, something that is everywhere and cannot be touched." I lost my train of thought then, staring off into the blankness of a bare white wall on the side.

"Ain't like you to shake like a damn leaf in a hurricane. You know I don't want you to get a big head, but you're one of our best dogs. You have this fire, this spark that has surpassed and charged through so much. You've been through a lot of shit, kid, and yet you pull through, loyal to our cause, ready to nuke all these abominations. You've got the stuff. So, just barrel though this bastard with everything you got. You can use all the weapons you need, but stop sulking; I hate seeing that weak little girl look on you." He nodded at me, firm and final. His speech touched me and confused me a bit. Our teams knew about the strength of the *lamia*, but luckily not the fact there was a human follower with him. I'm not sure how Galen would react to that news, but it surely made things complicated.

His pep talk inspired me to ask a burning question I had wanted to ask for years. "Galen . . . How'd you get your scar?"

You could hear the silence in the room become deafening, the wisps of steam coming from our cups our only companion. I waited patiently as I stared into his eyes. The scar seemed to become bolder as if it was yearning to either answer or flee from my question, from its backstory.

"Well lass, that's a shitty tale, one that don't have a happy ending like your fluffy House of Mouse junk, but, I suppose it's a bonding sort of night, now eh?" He took a large intake of breath and then whisked me away into a trip to the past:

"When I was a young man, I was in the military. I'm from the country lands outside of Erie, Pennsylvania, fifth generation of soldier in my family and damn proud of it. The thrill of killing a sick bastard, hitting my mark, shooting a gun, sword combat, wrestling, karate . . . it has all both fascinated or come easy to me since I was a wee one. May sound gross to you, sweetie pie, but that is how I am.

"I enjoyed getting into the thicket of conflict for what was right, mostly in dangerous countries where wars and dictators reigned. I was able to climb up to international special ops ranking at twenty-seven. I got to travel to Europe and Asia, going on missions, training, killing lowlives, saving prisoners, and interacting with an array of lovely ladies . . ." He gave me a wink and a deep rumbling in his throat that could only be satisfaction.

I rolled my eyes. "El grosso. Old man sex is not what I want to hear right now. Continue with the brutal killing, please."

He rested his head on his fist, propping it up to give me an intimidating snark and a "you don't know what you're missing" expression. "Don't flatter yourself, sweetheart, and I was pretty legendary. Barmaids knew my reputation the second I walked in a tavern. . . ." His face got wistful and arrogant, him mentally reliving his glory days apparent.

I merely snorted and looked at him until he moved on, "I did this for ten years, getting as many scars as I did medals and honors. What a ride it all was. I ended up in England, a bloody conflict the government wanted to keep hushed between some rivaling families. It was stupid, really, something about missing lambs they owned, but the carnage was getting intense. So, our unit went into the fray, a third group to look scary with our muscles and massive guns. We agreed to meet with both groups in an open field. It was exceedingly windy that day and I remember I was laser focused, thinking about Romona, a lovely tavern girl I was starting to get serious with. Her place wasn't too far from where we were and I swore I could smell her cinnamon-kissed skin.

"I didn't think we would encounter anything major as we marched forward, getting sight of the small laughable armies that these too rich families came from both sides of us, their expressions stoned-face, but fear was swirling all in their eyes. We stood there, boulders of justice for the government. We knew we could snuff them out easily if they were disagreeable. But, that's when the sky changed.

"It became red, blood red. The scent of rage could almost be tasted and the air was thick, the wind slicing through your ribs. It was hard to see through the violent gales. All of us looked up to see a cloaked figure, a tattered heap of horror that was looming and descending down from the skies. Some sort of demented crow beasts were flying alongside it, flanking it. As this creature got closer into my line of sight, I saw its hands were glistening, near blinding—"

"Did it . . . this *monstrum*, have a figure like . . . a woman?" I choked out, having trouble finding my voice.

A lump clearly could be seen in Galen's throat, "Yes. It was hard to see much from the distance with the deep gray shredded and holy cloak that was flowing around her. Once she swooped in closer, I saw she was a blue-faced hag, stringy seaweed and gray hair, and the fiercest, blood-lust filled eyes I had ever seen. The smell of rotting flesh radiated all around the open space, but I knew it came from her; her tongue and teeth were blood-stained. But what caught your attention was her claws, more like massive talons made out of—"

"Iron." I finished the statement. My hands became glued together and went under my chin, the scene unfolding around me as if I was in the battle with Galen.

It was hard to shock the weapon's master, but Galen's mouth opened a bit, the look he gave me unreadable. "You know your stuff there, kid. Makes me feel sad for you sometimes cause you're stuck in this business."

"Doesn't seem like you had a choice either." I searched his eye, a new-found respect for him bubbling inside me, his scar the one badge of honor he never predicted he would gain. "I never would have guessed you were the one that survived the Black Annis..."

"Yeah. 'Black Anna' is a bitch." He put one of her nicknames in air quotes. "Well, you're sharp enough to know the rest. It was so fast. She cut torsos in half like a knife to butter, skinning the flesh and hanging them from her belt, munching on slivers of skin between quick kills as her crows pecked eyes and broken bones with sickening delight. She slurped blood staring at her lifeless victim, her metal claws blinking in crimson light that matched the still too red sky. She took out those petty high-class boys like they were nothing; they didn't even have time to flee and their screams were cut-off before they could barely begin." He shook his head fiercely, as if he was trying to smack the image from his memories.

"Our men were frozen, watching in unexplainable horror as she nose-dived at our direction, taking out the back ranks like they were bowling pins. And then it was an all-out war: we fired guns, grenades, a few brave SOBs charged and tried daggers. She was just too fast and would swipe them away with her too massive claws. One-by-one, I watched my men fall, men who had survived so many wars, battles, ambushes... I didn't know what the Hell I was looking at. It took all of me to keep my gun steady.

"In all the madness, I didn't know the crow things had left and it was just me, alone, staring down this abomination. Time stopped, my chest beating in my ears and all I could focus on was the red world behind her and the snark of delight she was showing by baring her blood-soaked teeth. She made the first move, it so swift I could barely track her. I took a few shots of my automatic, but I either missed or she deflected them like bugs. And then she was in front of me and for the first time in my life, I truly felt I was staring my death in the face. Boy, it was fucking ugly. The thought of being wiped out by a witchy thing I didn't understand lit a fuse in my ass, allowing me to move at the last second from a fatal blow in the chest, but... she still got my eye, her iron claws grazing me, digging deep into my flesh.

"God, all I saw was red, my face warm and sticky. My muscles were trembling and my knees caved in on me. Through the heavy breathing and extreme pain, I sent a general prayer to whatever divine being would care for an asshole like me, prepping for her to zoom in to devour me. But, I was greeted instead with a smacking sound and what I assumed was her cackling, although it sounded like she was choking on a cat. I struggled, but was able to look up to see that her crow minions were back and they had dragged over more bodies for her to feast on. The only place that was even near the field was the tavern I visited often . . .

"And in her right grip . . . was Romona."

I gasped outwardly, covering my mouth with my hands to try to stop my tears that yearned to be shed. Most of us here had tragedies in our lives involving *monstrum*, but the shocking and grotesque stories don't get easier to swallow. Some parts of our hearts have to crystallize, but I think the rest of it tenderizes and absorbs each other's sorrows and losses.

Galen exhaled some hard air, his voice getting a slight rasp to it, "Black Annis hovered a few feet off the ground, her head swooping down to clank her sharp teeth together, burning her gaze right into me. I tried to call out, but pain still had snagged me and my voice was failing. And Romona was out cold, limp in her talon. I was able to twitch my fingers to try to reach her, but the bitch knew how to scar me further: with one squeeze, she snapped my love in half, her guts and blood spattering all over the field and watering the ground. The crack of her spine echoed across the open space. Then, it tried to speak, a look of crazed, elated hunger on her face as she scooped up a decent-sized bloody clump that had come out with the pile of guts and intestines. By the time I processed what that precious clump was, Black Annis swallowed it whole and howled in glee, she somehow taking everything I had, known and unknown, in one attack.

"The only human like word I heard it spoke as she licked her claws dripped in blood were . . . 'baby . . .'"

Oh no . . . Oh no, no, no . . . I shook my head rapidly, my hair whipping my neck, I trying to feel even a small percentage of pain that loss must have caused Galen, his lover scattered in pieces like broken toys at his feet. His voice hushed, but wove me into its web once more.

"So . . . I lashed out. I guess bored or finished, she tossed the pieces of the girl I wanted to get to truly know better and care for, I stood and reached into my belt for something, anything, I hadn't tried yet. And then, when she was in my face within striking distance, where a hunk of innards from my Romona were stuck in her teeth, I swiped with all my might with the one thing I had left: a sharpened, steady stake made of oak I had made out of boredom on one of our walks through the UK countryside."

My heart leapt out of my chest, realizing his luck for his life or some shitty form of fate that made him a true Hunter. "That was damn lucky. The Black Annis lives and stalks her fleshy prey by an oak tree. Some myths say she was born from that tree. So, that would have been the best weapon to do real damage."

"And I bloody did! Her face had a scar to match mine and it burned, sizzled loudly, steam pouring out profusely as she howled and backed away. I was in my own rage mode and kept lazily slashing with that oak stick. I'm not even sure if she was getting hit, but she sure hated it and smoke was seeping out of her, even her crows getting quiet. In clouds of dark smoke, she flew away, although it was a challenge for her. After that, I remember falling to my knees after trying to talk into my walkie, but I ended up waking up in a Hunters van and staring into the face of a Ms. Beryl Edric, a feisty, no-shits woman, like she is today."

I shared a small smile with Galen, my image of a Chief ten years younger when she was climbing the ranks a small glimmer of light in this dark story. My hands gripped my cup tightly, my nails digging into the styrofoam. I wanted to snuff out that bitch who did this to Galen, ring her neck and pop off her head. Especially for eating Romona's own fetus, a new life that never got a chance to grow. That tore my heart in two.

Galen leaned back on the tall chair and put his arms behind his head, acting all cool as if the story he just told me was nothing. "Does that answer your question, kid? And I don't want any pouts or pity or I will make you do one-hundred lunges before you have to go to work tomorrow!"

I rolled my eyes to try to hide the tears that wanted to leak from my eyes again. I better listen or the bastard would. And lunges freakin hurt. "No pity here. We all have a past. I am glad I understand you better. And I have to admit, the fact you pushed through it and stayed yourself is pretty remarkable. Maybe I'll join your fanclub now, Captain."

"Oh Lord, keep your panties in your skirt, missy. Not interested in nerdy little girls that like that Hi Cat thing."

"It's *Hello Kitty*, you insensitive ass." I smacked his bicep and he crinkled his cup and tossed it at me. We both decided it was time for bed, cleaning up our table in a thoughtful silence. It was three by then and going home now would be a stupid choice, so I went to check-out a small cot room, another convenience for long, odd hour missions. I grabbed fresh beddings and a pair of basic PJs from the laundry mat, needing to rest my eyes and praying I didn't see flashbacks of Galen's past, or of, perhaps, my own—

"*Siyo*, my child." A feathery voice entered my ears before I turned my rented room handle. I turned to see the pleasant figure of Mrs. Adsila Edric, the mother of my esteemed Chief and the Wise Medical Woman of her Cherokee tribe. She was adorned in a traditional tribal white gown with matching leather fringe everywhere, a beaded yellow and red sun with black detailing around it. Her gray and chestnut tone hair was braided in an elaborate twist, a simple white headband with red squares sewn all over it. In her hands, I noticed a bundle of lavender stalks.

"Good night to you, Madame Edric." I bowed respectfully, my fist over my heart as we exchanged a tender smile. I deeply admired Madame Edric and all her wisdom, amazing spiritual intonations, and tender compassion for us. Nothing slowed her down and she never gave up on the fight for good, her sharp mind and sensing abilities helping our organization time and time again.

She cradled her lavender slightly closer to her and then reached over to lightly pat my hand, her weathered, but gentle touch easing me into a feeling of calm. There truly was a grandmotherly feel to her in every way. "Oh please, dearest. You know I don't need to be called Madame. It makes me sound snobbish."

Her statement was ended with her sticking out her tongue and I chuckled in reply.

"Anyway, I was dropping off some more lavender to the intervention rooms. I am glad Beryl incorporates it in the methods here. Lavender is so soothing for the mind and soul. Although, my husband just likes me to use it in cookies when he goes golfing with his business buddies. Maybe that's all an old woman is good for?!" She covered her mouth, trying not to get tickled. Mr. Edric was a CEO for a major international company that dealt with fine quality gemstones for jewelry stores. He is very fierce and not afraid to tackle a problem, always efficient. Chief got her director attitude from him and her independence and acceptance of the supernatural from her mother.

"I haven't seen you in a while, Valda. I hear you are burning your candle at both ends with this latest assignment?"

It was a challenge to not roll my eyes at the thought of working with Hot Dog Brain, but I restrained myself. "We do have a difficult and quite unique assignment right now and are resourcing out, which is rare. I'm doing my best as always. It's been a long night and I figured resting my eyes for a bit here would be safer than risking driving." A reassuring smile spread on my face on its own when I noticed Madame Edric's look of concern despite her still angelic smile. "I'll be alright, promise. But, if lavender can help stop a *lamia*, I appreciate that help."

"Ha, oh my, well, I am not sure about that, but I can surely give you some lavender to calm your nerves tonight to get some rest." She took a small bud and tucked it behind my ear, the delicate smell making me glad.

"Thank you very much. I know this will help." I bowed to her again.

I was getting ready to turn the knob to say good night, when her voice halted my advances, "Valda, when you think of change, what color do you see?"

Confused, I cocked my head a bit, my gears trying to answer the odd question honestly. "Well, the one I see is yellow."

"Hm . . . a good choice. Now, why do you think this?" Her look was kind and patient, as if I was taking the most important test in the world and she was supportive of my answer.

"Be . . . because the wind is always changing and for some reason, when I close my eyes, that's the color I see the wind wants to be . . ." My cheeks became warm and I felt bashful, giving her this answer.

"That is fitting for the way you soar, Valda. And it is interesting to me to see you said the same color he did." The words hung in the space around us, the air of mystery intense and thick.

The curiosity baited me into a trap, the one this wise woman had laid out, "Who?"

"Why, Wren of course." Her toothy smile gave me the illusion that she was toying with my shocked expression and enjoying my naive nature.

"Mr. Stillman?" I wasn't even sure why this surprised me, but the fact I could have something so abstract in common with Mr. Stillman partly flattered me, but also offended me, him being the leader of The Bringers and all that. I still didn't know why this question was brought up or even mattered, but it was Madame Edric asking and I trusted her judgement.

"Yes indeed, *Uwetsiageya*. When I first met Wren, only a few days after the incident that brought him to the supernatural, he was indeed scarred by the experience, like anyone would be, but his resolve, his spirit, although buried deep in sadness, was still staying afloat. He was thinking, thinking of the next steps, how to incorporate this into his life. Even in trauma, he knew he could not erase what happened, knew there was no running away. He honored what he lost by thinking and keeping his soul above the crying feelings his heart wanted to drown in. But he still loved and hurt desperately, no doubt on that. He just had such an inner strength, be it quiet at first, but he attempted change even at the worst time."

I nodded, my heart aching once more for a fellow person affected by the *monstrums'* savagery. Inside, I had always thought Mr. Stillman had ended up in his chair from a *monstrum* attack. I knew he had been in charge of The Bringers for eight years after only joining the group a year before that. He and the Chief both became in charge not too far off, although Chief had been a field agent like me, dedicated to The Hunters for a while before that. Like with Galen's tale, knowing the background of how someone was hurt by the *monstrum* was hard to stomach and always made your nerves buzz with sorrow and head spin with rage.

I swallowed hard, having trouble looking Madame in her warm eyes. "Who . . . who did he lose? His wife?" I knew he had been married, but lately, I hadn't heard much of her.

"No, his daughter. The three of them were on vacation together to celebrate her twenty-first birthday before she graduated with her bachelor's in liberal science early. They were on the coast of Italy, a lovely resort by the ocean, when during a sudden, horrid storm, a group of *venti* attacked, drowning and tearing limb from limb several civilians with their stormy wings and strong electric eyes, blending into the gales to cause a cyclone. Cathy, his wife, was sunning and able to run to safety. Lydia however, was far from shore, swimming.

"Wren tried to get her, but was thrown like a rag doll, his back breaking in the process. He had to watch his precious child get sucked into the whirlwind and be shredded into pieces. With his gaze never leaving the scene, he was able to see the figures inside the wind and conclude they were not human. And the poor dear was engaged to be married to her childhood sweetheart. Truly, it was a tragedy.

"His wife was enraged with him, especially after he told her what he saw. They tried to make their marriage work for a few years even after he joined The Bringers, but she had enough and left. She died last year from breast cancer. Wren had no ill wishes towards her and they still were friends after the divorce. Wren is also still good friends with his almost son-in-law, whose a very successful business man. Through this whole ordeal, I best recall his spirit, even after losing so much, he saw the yellow of the wind, the candle we use to represent wind. You remind me of that Valda, with a similar spirit."

I blinked away the tears that were stinging my eyes, yearning to be shed. Mr. Stillman was always so kind. I felt guilty for knowing his story without his consent, but this made me see maybe all Bringers were not so bad, just more foolish to trust *monstrum* after they destroyed their lives. Jeremey was still a Dickwagon with a side of fries, but, to quote his pop princess Hannah Montana, nobody's perfect.

"I'll do my best, Madame Edric. Thank you for sharing your belief in me and the story. It is inspiring to be reminded of why we do all this sometimes." I tapped my lavender plant by my hair, loving its sweet scent. "And thank you for the gift. I will use it to get hopefully 90 minutes of sleep before work."

"Oh goodness! Look at me talk and talk. My apologies, little dove. Please get some rest. I will pray for your success in this mission and be on the lookout for anything to stop a blood sucker." We placed our fists over our hearts once more and bowed, a wave of affection washing over me. I will surely have to call my grandma tomorrow and discuss the philosophy and cuteness of Winnie the Pooh like we often do.

"It is always an honor. I know you are an owl in the light and a songbird that sings for the rising sun. I wish I had your dedication. I look forward to seeing you soon." A smile appeared on my face and I pushed open the door halfway to enter as I waved good-bye.

Before I was fully inside and she trotted away, I heard her holler to me, "Do not fear the Spiky One; he may be more than he appears."

Was she talking cryptically again or talking about Sir Ham-It-Up-A Lot? I smacked my cheeks to get out of that mindset, although his spikes were out of control. Still, I didn't want my last thought to be Jeremey before I drifted away to Dreamland. As I got situated for the night, I sniffed my lavender companion and tried to paint a better world with the yellow of my wind.

CHAPTER 9

Flowers bud. The weather changes. The sun rises and sets, the moon replacing it. People go through their daily routines. And that is what I did. Time stepped in, running its course at its own pace, just like it always did.

Life consisted of teaching my darling ducklings and setting up for our spring book fair with its Pinterest filled Under the Sea crafts. Then, there were all the meetings with my new 'boss' as I had to master the art of not vomiting when all my female comrades swooned and sighed. To add more to do, we had meetings with Chief and the team about the *lamia* case, I my regular Hunter's schedule, and the job of dodging Stupid Face's flirtations and advances. Overall, he was fairly quiet for him, subdued almost, but he would try to stroke my hair from behind often at Headquarters or wink at me with what he assumed was a sexy smile at staff meetings.

He was a thorn in my side, but I was slowly getting accustomed to the pain. He was wedged into my life and I knew no matter how hard I fought, I had to suck it up and do this for my organization, heck, even the world. Jeremey Darington was still an annoying, weird, self-absorbed bastard that made my skin crawl and made my fist want to punch anything in sight when I heard his smooth, arrogant, jock voice, but I was getting used to him.

We even, gag me for saying this, had lunch together. He went around and ordered everyone Subway to celebrate his first three weeks of being at our building. While the other teachers blushed and gushed about how kind he was, I was zoned, only thinking of free food. My daddy raised me right; never turn down free food.

When I was paged to his office right before our lunch break, his silky voice informed my kiddos and the passing Ms. Coleman's class in the hall that he wanted me to eat lunch with him in order to discuss the Reading for the Summer program, a committee I was truly the co-chairwoman of with the librarian. Lindsey gave me a look of congratulations and a hint of envy in her lovely sparkly eyes before walking past with her chickadees. My *hoshis* were thrilled for me, telling me that it was nice for their new, cool principal to invite me to lunch and that he must want to be my friend. My cheeks hurt from the tight, fake smile and forced laugh I had to show the little ones.

I arrived in his office, with the door wide open so Ms. Candyfloss could see our dining arrangement (thank the Lord; a witness). When I caught sight of him, he held up two bags filled with eat fresh goodness, a dazzling beam painted on his face. "Steak and bacon flatbread with mayo, ranch, tomato, cucumber, and lots of pickles along with a triple chocolate cookie for a treat?"

I gulped, stunned, but not because he knew my order. The Hunters got sandwiches a lot because it was quick and I only went between three sandwiches. He probably assumed I wanted meat today with all that was going on with our busy schedules and man, he was right. I was craving some meat!

Ms. Candyfloss had apparently passed out the other sandwiches earlier to the staff and took orders. Pretty brazen of Super Dork to think he knew my sandwich. The universe was lucky he got it right. He invited me to sit in a plush red chair with gold accents across from him and we ate in a comfortable bubble of slightly awkward, but casual and pleasant conversation.

It was odd, but I had to admit, it wasn't that bad, shooting the bull about school, media, and random, silly life stories over ranch and cucumbers.

There hadn't been any development in the *lamia* case, which was unnerving to me. Regardless, there were always things to do at the organization: debriefing, meetings with Kesler, where I tried to include Bonnie in our conversation whenever I could. I loved being gifted with his adorable cherry-hued face. Then work-out sessions, combat training, situational obstacle courses, counseling, self-defense ass-kicking classes with Galen, and the general monitoring of the supernatural with research. We now had to share the space with about five Bringers that Mr. Stillman had selected to help with our *lamia* cause. It was foreign passing them in the hall, my lips puckering on their own because I was trying not to frown or glare. I didn't want The Hunters getting a rep of being rude, just butt-kicking and powerful.

Time kept on flowing in every aspect of my existence, just like it exactly should have the day Rickey strolled into the base.

"*Hola*, my lovely *senorita*! How I have missed you, Ms. Valda!"

The exclamation spoken in a honey, energetic tone with an adorable and alluring Spanish accent came from the far left side of the open space of the computer area. I turned towards it, surprised to see Rickey Aguinaldo, a familiar person for me once a month at the Headquarters. A smile appeared on my face as I soaked in his young, handsome features that were running towards me. Per the norm, he wore an insanely tight black t-shirt and jeans, biker boots, and leather cuffs with Spanish words written all over them. Rickey once told me they were inspirational quotes.

I walked forward a bit to welcome him with a firm handshake and warm smile, but he turned my hand over and brushed his soft lips on my flesh. I tried not to react, but I had to admit, he was charming, unlike some prickly-haired airheads I knew. Rickey really was a doll.

Too bad he was six years younger than me.

"Hiya Rickey. It's great to see you. Are you here doing your rounds?"

He displayed his pearly whites before replying, "Yeah. Dad sent me in his place. Ms. Edric is coming up to greet me. I am so happy I got to see you though." He looped his arm through mine after nudging his cheek on my own playfully. "Valda, I'm so lucky to run into you. Now, you can give me the inspection tour. And then we can go on a date!" His excitement to spend time with me was sweet, but I really had work to do.

"That will not be needed, Mr. Aguinaldo. I am here to assist you as usual." Chief strode up in her clicking heels with four guards flanking her, although her professional gaze could rip steel. She was used to dealing with Rickey and his family. When Rickey saw Chief, he slid his hand down my arm and then let his arm swing between the small space between us, a windmill slowly falling off its bolts. I tried not to snicker at his let down face that he attempted to firm up to show he was an adult, there doing official business. It's like Chief stole all his fun.

"An honor to see you again, Chief Edric." Rickey nodded politely, taking a step towards her.

Chief returned his greeting with a short head bob of her own. "Indeed, it is. How is your father? I read about his new venture of merging with Apple on a fairly impressive project." Not surprising that Chief kept tabs on all modern affairs, even those with business. I struggled with this person-ally, unless it was about Japanese media, pop culture, and entertainment. I shine there.

"Yeah, it's pretty exciting to be teaming up with Apple; he'll get us a lot of money from this partnership, so of course he's good." I rolled my eyes at the ceiling and gave Chief a smirk when our eyes met. She wanted to groan from the expression she gave back to me. Rickey loved the rich, comfy life his family had set-up for him. I imagined him sitting on an arm chair made of large bills in his spare time, while playing the latest games and watching his servants go down a slip-n-slide that was installed in his bedroom.

When my eyes once again focused on the conversation at hand, I caught sight of Jeremey strolling into the area, all casual like he owned this place now. Sicko. He stopped short behind one of the guards surrounding Chief, puzzlement filling his sea-green hues. Still, Jeremey kept his lazy grin on his face as he soaked up the scene in front of him. Mr. Stillman soon rolled in and took the spot beside Jeremey, having his kind, grandfather smile when he entered.

Chief pushed her glasses up, collecting herself before speaking to Rickey again, "Well, Mr. Aguinaldo, I know your time is precious, so let us begin with our tour—"

"Heya Val! Ready for our debriefing with Kyler, my sweetness?"

The sound of his shout made my lips pucker in annoyance. Rickey stopped his foot he had lifted up in mid-air from moving forward. Our onlookers turned to gawk at us, but Meathead didn't show any notice or care at all about this.

My muscles tightened and a small headache was forming in my temple. I pushed this out of the way to holler back to him, irritation hard to hide in my face and tone, "It's Kesler, Mr. Insensitive. And I was on my way...." My breath felt hot, trying to be professional with an audience when I was talking to the King of Stupidity.

Chief turned to face Jeremey and Mr. Stillman, her lethal glare making even Monkey Brains gulp loudly and wince. Mr. Stillman just kept on smiling, as if this was an entertaining comedy routine. "Mr. Darington, Ms. Hemmingway was assisting me in helping a very important guest to our Headquarters. She is excused for her tardiness and I recommend you let us conduct our business in the manner The Hunters see fit."

Jeremey tripped all over his words, seeming foolish enough that you could near see it on his crisp white shirt, like an ugly mustard stain, "Ye... Yes ma'am." Mr. Stillman chuckled, giving Jeremey an understanding look, but I loved Chief's cut-throat, no BS in her business style. This is why we were amazing in comparison to The Bringers. Suck on that egg, Darington!

Rickey stood there, his eyes squinted and face tight as he looked at Jeremey. "Valda... who is that cocky prick in the white shirt? He doesn't seem like a new Hunter or someone you should be associated with." Oh, how right the boy was.

"Umm ... well ..." I looked at Chief, who had joined the bubble of conversation with me and Rickey, my eyes pleading for help in explaining this odd and stressful situation. We did not want to piss off the Aguinaldo family and I knew this was a delicate matter.

Chief picked up on my cue and answered for me, "Mr. Darington is from The Bringers. We have been working with a select, top-notch group of them on some serious disappearing cases. It is not ideal, but we must protect the mortals in any way we can. Mr. Wren Stillman and myself are foreseeing over the assignment and will keep things in a strict line."

Rickey's tanned face began to pale from shock, it giving him an odd coloring. He was silent for several long pauses, staring and assessing every angle of Jeremey he could see, who was chatting up Mr. Stillman like nothing abnormal had happened.

When Rickey spoke, his voice was raspy and thick, it adding twenty years to him it felt, "Valda is too good to work with such a pansy who is trying to compensate for something. Don't worry about my family cutting ties with The Hunters, but Valda being forced to work with such an ass is degrading and a disservice to her. I hope the old man stays in line!" Rickey shouted that last sentence across the area and gave daggers to the man who was dishonoring me, supposedly.

Jeremey perked up, arching his eyebrow with a gentle curiosity at Rickey. My young pal squeezed my hand protectively and with tender affection before maturely turning away. "Let's go ahead and begin my inspection, Chief Edric." He briskly exited, Chief and her guards clicking away at a fast pace to keep up with him, hastily beginning their tour.

"Geez. What the hell is that little guy's problem?" I had been watching the group walk away so I hadn't heard Dork-R-Us come up behind me, his easy smile looking like that of a movie star's staring off dreamily into the distance in a romantic classic.

I sighed, the fire gradually being snuffed out of me. I felt this needed to be explained in a serious manner, "Rickey is the son of Mr. Augustin Aguinaldo, the billionaire business tycoon. They are related to Emilio

Aguinaldo, the youngest Philippine President and the first president of the constitutional republic of Asia. They have Spanish-American War generals on both sides of the war through marriage and they have always been very successful and rich. The past three generations of the Aguinaldo family have financially supported The Hunters heavily in our research, equipment, and training resources. Once a month, either Augustin or Rickey now that he is older comes to inspect what we have been doing with their funds and how it is helping The Hunters help the world. They are investors and we have to treat them with the utmost respect to help keep us running. Don't you Bringers have investors too?"

For our whole conversation I had been looking off into the distance too, allowing the importance to flow out of me, until the last sentence, when I looked at him quizzically. Jeremey raised his brow again, searching my face before replying, "Yeah, but they are crusty old men that don't fawn over beautiful, older women; only whistling at them from afar, like real professionals."

"Hm . . . not surprising that all of you Bringers, besides Mr. Stillman, are pigs." I mumbled, not even meeting his eyes.

"Oh, Father Stillman, to paraphrase the goddess Britney Spears, isn't so innocent. You forget he's a man and was young once. He doesn't mind us having fun as long as we keep it clean." An admiring smile glowed on Pig-Goat's face.

My head turned to look at Mr. Stillman on its own, a pang hitting my chest recalling his story about his losing the women in his life, yet he still continued to stay strong. He caught my glance and twittered his fingers at me in a friendly little wave that I returned shyly. This kind man was chatting up the guard like nothing was different between our groups and there is still good in the world. I wish I could see through those rose-colored glasses once again, like before I knew of *monstrum*, but that seems like a fantasy now.

Jack-on-Crack randomly put his arm around my shoulder loosely, inhaling deeply as I stared menacingly as his fingers wrapped around me.

"It's all pretty crazy, isn't it? This roller coaster of a job we have to somehow hide while protecting all the little people below? We will get this vampire bastard Val and I'll protect you so you can shine in glory like you're meant to."

This face was casual, his eyes singing with confidence, his touch tender, but protective as he looked onward. As much as it hurt me to admit, his words slightly spellbound me and made me feel safe, like I could believe them. I wasn't sure why he said them and at this certain moment, but I could surely believe them—

"Get your hand off her!" I jumped a bit at the loud boom that erupted almost too far off in front of me for me to see. Jeremey shrugged and let go in a hip manner, crossing his arms to appear to be the coolest cat at the jukebox. A devilish little twinkle sparked in his iris, but an annoyed twitch appeared in his left eye.

An enraged Rickey was Godzilla stomping at a very fast speed towards us, Chief calling after him in a near sprint (for what can be a sprint in heels), her face pinkish. The boy didn't slow down and got right up close to us, a mere foot from our bubble as he shot hatred up at Jeremey with his scowl alone. It was just a stare down, a nonverbal testosterone battle I didn't understand at all. You could feel the heat crackling around them, the hairs on my arm rising and my neck tensing.

"Look, *old man*. I get you have to work with Valda to save mankind and all that bullshit, but you don't have the right to touch her. Why would she want a grandpa trying to relive his juggernaut, empty-headed football days when she could have someone who can provide for her? I'm a cocoa-brown delight and you're a pasty, pansy can of paint. So, my suggestion is, if you want The Hunters to benefit then get lost!"

The fury in Rickey's eyes could have burnt toast on impact, his fists tightening against his jeans after his rant. He had become a young Cyclops defending Jean Gray and his laser vision was not going to stay hidden, but instead blast it straight in Darington's face, branding an R into his flesh. I wouldn't put it past this new side of Rickey, one that caught me off-guard. Everyone else in the room, even roamers stopped to take in the scene, the raised voices, and still two glaring baboons. I could have sworn I heard a scientist and one of Jeremey's Bringer brothers betting. Good night, *Kamisama*!

Jeremey rebutted, his teeth mashing and breathing getting quicker, a steaming volcano allowing its lava inside to boil, "Wow. Bullshit. Such foul language. Does your mommy need to wash your mouth out with soap young man?" His eyes narrowed as he tapped Rickey's head, ruffling his bangs slightly. You could almost hear the room collectively gasp, Rickey's arm near swatted Jeremey's hand away, but like The Bringer he was, he dodged it with lightning reflexes.

A heartless chuckle escaped Mr. Bringing the Awkwardness lips. "Listen Junior; Ms. Hemmingway is a powerful, independent woman that don't need no man, but if she wanted one, I think that's her choice and let me tell you ... Why would she want a little boy who just graduated from Underoos and wears too much musky aftershave when she can have a real man, Richie Rich? Yes, your daddy has funds, but that can't make up for a lack of other assets"

That's it! After my ears stop whistling like a freight train and my eyes can see any color besides red that I bet matches my blush, both of these 'men' are gonna get their Johnny's chopped off by a cleaver!

Both Chief and I opened our mouths, her expression matching how I felt. Oh, they were gonna get it, two blades hacking from both sides, but Rickey beat us to the punch. "You don't have the history or chemistry we do! I've been coming here with my father for six years and Valda has always been kind to me. We are made for each other. Come on!" My wrist was suddenly being grabbed and I was dragged to the center of the vast computer room by a fuming Rickey. "We will show you! Play some music for us to dance to, a tango!" Rickey demanded with a flourishing snap, talking to one of the stunned staff members.

"Oh hell. This is ridiculous ..." I heard Chief moan, exasperated and about on the edge of losing her cool from the slight crazed look in her eyes.

"Hey slick?! Who were you named after? Rickey Ricardo? If that's the case, you can Bob-a-loo right on out of here." Jeremey was heckling now, but Rickey's reply was to squeeze my waist, pressing our chests near each other as our hands embedded together. Jeremey's jaw squared so hard that I was scared it would smash and break, his eyes blazing, a circle of gold etching itself around his pupils.

"Wait! Umm, listen, Rickey, this is silly. I'm not a very good dancer and this . . . really isn't the place for it . . ." My nerves were frying, my brain in panic mode of how I could get out of this. I really wasn't a good natural dancer, but more of a learn choreography after weeks of training with fellow theater peeps dancer. I also didn't like how Jeremey was glaring at us either. He had moved against the wall, crossing his arms, his neck throbbing and his jaw still so tight I worried we would have to pry it open.

"How to be a Heartbreaker" blurred through the speakers. Rickey raised our arms and began to sway me masterfully, twirling me in elegant circles, his feet light and skilled at following the beats. I tried to follow along, but I was stepping all over myself and Rickey's shoes, trying to balance myself and not fall on my face. Rickey even had to catch me in his arms twice, spinning me to make it look like it was a dance move.

I felt like a large klutz, especially compared to Rickey, who I knew had had tango lessons since he was seven. We have danced and waltzed a few times for fun at the Headquarters, but doing this in front of an audience was making me mess up more, my faults out there for all I respected to see. My stomach shook with dread and I prayed my face wasn't tomato red, but I'm sure it was, matching my bugged-out eyes too well.

"I'm here for you Ms. Valda. Just watch me and we can become one together. You don't need that dog." Rickey had such confidence in me that it touched my heart, but that didn't lighten my embarrassment at all. I didn't even know why these boys were being *bakas*. How medieval backwards they were acting. I'm my own knight in shining armor, except for right now. How I wanted to break out from this dance.

"Mind if I cut in?" Grateful for the save, I turned to smile at my savior, but my face dropped when I saw it was Jerk and Beans. His bright eyes were full of fury, but his grin was warm and focused on me.

"You can't do that grandpa! Go get your adult diapers and buzz off!" Rickey howled angrily, his arms moving to my shoulders.

Jeremey leaned closer until his forehead was touching mine, but his nose was pointing at Rickey, his glare at the young man deadly. In a hot whisper, he warned, "Valda is not ready to be a cougar, little man." And leaving Rickey speechless, I was whisked away once more, this time pulled into the arms of Darington. The beam he gave me was affectionate, his eyes caring and only looking at me again. Still, I saw the hint of gold around the sea-green eyes, making their usual comforting luster dull and slightly sinister.

"Rule Number #3: Wear your heart on your cheek . . ."

The second verse of the song was beginning. As if following instructions, Jeremey stroked my cheek, his fingers as light as a feather, acting like I was made of precious glass. "Shall we show these people how graceful you are, Val?"

"Val?!" Rickey screamed, upset by overhearing Jeremey calling me by my name, a name that usually only my family called me. "How dare you be so informal to your superior?"

Hearing Val come out of Jeremey's mouth was odd, but I shook it off, deciding to sort out my feelings about it later. "Follow me Val, like we did at the club. Trust me; I will protect you." He interrupted my thoughts with those words I wanted to believe again.

As the music swelled, Jeremey clutched my hips, our bodies only mere inches apart as I looked into his face, trying to calm my thudding heartbeat so no one would hear. I took one step after allowing Jeremey to guide me, his hand my anchor. We moved in sync for a few bars, my legs growing more sure and steady. Our breathing became one, our pulses matching as we moved and swayed, my body confident to let him dip me once.

Once I was lifted backup to a standing position, trying not to be thrilled that for a moment, I felt like a princess, I examined Agent Smooth Steps once more. His look had softened and was only searching for me. "You're getting a little too close for my liking bud. This isn't like the assignment we had at the club; people here know us and hold us in a high rank and expect us to act in a respectful manner."

A tug landed on the tips of my long hair, not too far from my butt. He playfully twisted it through his finger, making it swing a little as he lightly held on to it like the reigns of a prized horse. "Darling, I'd take you right here, right now. The dance is an art, an expression for two people to harmonize their bodies, allowing their chemistry to build. And you are following me much better than The First Time Shaver over there, so I know you can handle more love."

A gag sound came out of my mouth as my ire at him began to flare up again. My knee went up to ram his groin, but stopped short by half an inch, my eyes giving him a warning. I liked having this level of control. I was greeted with a smirk that showed he seemed amused at this so called game. "Oh, my dear. I would be careful putting your knee on Bruno. He's already about bursting with lust for you. Don't think having your lovely self rubbing against him will keep him hush-hush."

"My God! You are the worst, mother—" My temper spiked, but I didn't get to move any further to crush Bruno with my kneecap like I dreamt. Before I could even breathe, he placed my leg that had my knee that was near his crotch attached to it. In one smooth motion, he next grabbed my inner thigh, wrapping it around his waist, and lifting me up with ease. We spun in a graceful circle on the floor we made our own, my fear sinking down into an abyss because I knew he would hold onto me, protect me.

Our peanut gallery cackled, hooted, gasped, or clapped. Mr. Stillman whistled loudly and praised us with utter glee. The Bringers were verbally worshipping their fellow brother like he was a god. Chief slapped her hand hard on her forehead, looking like she was about to rip her ponytail from its roots. Her legs were shaking, most likely with rage because her face made it look like she was going to blow her top. I'm glad I wasn't in the splash zone.

"Was that really called for?" I puckered my lips out, my eyes thinning at him.

"Would you like me to grab your delicious booty instead?" He winked at me, licking his lips a smidgen so they shone as much as the glint in his eyes. I swore I saw a sliver of liquid gold slithering around his pupils and amber flashing behind them. Still, his attention was only on me. I felt this pull too, this aura that seemed to be drawing us to each other, and like magnets, it was hard to get away from its hold. I felt lost, but home at the same time, fuzzy goosebumps forming on my skin. It was dizzying.

He grabbed my wrist once more and spun me with the art of a ballerina, making my heart leap with surprise and excitement that I could be as graceful as a swan, even if only for a split second. The crowd cheered wildly, especially Mr. Stillman, exclaiming "That's my boy!" over and over again.

Sausage Head gave his admirers a wave, thanking them for the support like he was a new star that had just magically won the Academy Award. Laughing, I informed him, "You're such an asshole, Darington."

"As long as I get to be yours, then it's a good time for me." A wave of understanding washed over me after I caught his wink. My face was becoming flushed, like I had been out in the sun just a few minutes too long. That's what Jeremey was; the sun. There were times he would hide, times I could avoid him, but I could never shake him off. Often, he burnt me and other times, he encouraged me to grow and brought a ray of light into my day. This man was always watching me, near stalking, but looking at him right now, sharing a smirk like we knew a secret only the two of us could, my insides warmed up. Jeremey Darington was fascinating me.

The song finished, my ears regaining sound and taking in colors again that did not belong to the partner I was forced to lock an embrace with. I felt like I was waking up from a dream. I saw Chief marching towards us, her angry footprint almost visible on the tile, but Rickey sprinted (doing a near *Naruto* run and forming dust clouds) past her to get up in Jeremey's business.

"I see that Ms. Valda trusts you, so for now, as a man, I'll concede. But..." And so clique that I wanted to bury my head like an ostrich, Rickey jabbed his finger in Jeremey's chest, who just stood there in mild surprise, Superman trying not to mock a poke from a child throwing a tantrum. "You'll be nothing to her beyond a forced upon her cohort. Get that through your muscle-bound brain. The Aguinaldos would make a powerful enemy..."

Tension once again set in Jeremey's jaw, harder than before. This time, I feared his bones would break from the pressure. He stuffed his fists forcefully in his beige dress pants, his attempt to look chill failing, his hunching back and rocking on his heels shattering that facade. The urge to say something was written on every inch of his face, enough to make my heart go out to him a bit. I didn't like this fight over male dominance, with me as the fake trophy. To quote my homegirl, Princess Jasmine, I am not a prize to be won. Still, words can hurt, doubt seeping into the marrow of your bones from others envy and harshness. Even the annoying Jeremey didn't deserve to go spiraling into these twisted feelings that were making him lose his composure.

"Mr. Darington, Mr. Stillman is needing to speak to you. *Now...*" Chief's voice commanded the whole room, but the words were in a whisper that was only heard by the four of us. The glare she was aiming straight at Jeremey was pissed and told him that she *would* deal with him later. Don't want to be at the receiving end of that target practice.

He gave a formal salute to Chief, a charming smile painting on his face. "Yes, Mrs. Edric." Then he clicked his heels together and pivoted to walk to the wall where Mr. Stillman was sitting.

A sigh popped out of Chief's red-lips before she sternly gazed at me and Rickey. "Shall we finish the inspection properly, Mr. Aguinaldo? You sort of rushed through the left corridor. Ms. Hemmingway? I hate to impose on your time, but could you join us before you go to your already late meeting with Mr. Darington and Kesler?" She turned to me, tired, motherly affection on her face, a near pleading expression in her eyes.

"Of course, Chief." I put a fist over my heart and gave her a slight bow, then spinning on my heels to do the same to our guest, Rickey, a greeting smile on my face. "Will you allow me to join you for this inspection, Rickey?"

He nearly hopped with excitement, but stopped before he fully blasted off, worry creasing his brow and a puppy pout gracing his admittedly lush looking lips. "Valda, I'm still your little werewolf, right?"

This tickled me and I patted his hair, stroking his sideburns teasingly, him feeling like he was a buff, more manly little brother. I had told Rickey when I first met him that he reminded me of Jacob Black from my beloved *Twilight* series, when he still had his long hair. I still saw him as that, a loveable young man I knew was my friend, even if he was clingy at times. Why do I always get the clingy ones?

"Ha, ha! Yes. You'll always be my Jacob, you handsome werewolf…" Rickey beamed widely, giving me a seductive, but still adorable look.

"Come on Valda; let's go on a date after this inspection. You know, there is this new Marvel movie I've been wanting to see…" And as I was being tugged away by the wrist, my young suitor droning on and on, my eyes caught sight of Jeremey. He was leaning against the wall, his well-pressed shirt making him nearly blend in.

The face I saw was set in a firm line, but his eyes were wide, soaking up the image of Rickey and I getting further away. I felt like I was looking at a man of stone and a man who was broken, and I was his lifeline that was being taken from his grasp. Jeremey was my enemy, a Bringer, a pervert, an annoyance, my imposter boss…

But I wanted to reach out to him.

"Yo! Darington?!" I yelled, his ears perking up like a battered dog hearing his master, "I'll see you at our debriefing with Kesler in ten minutes. So, quit being a prick and high tail it over there, unless you need me to beat you in something else!"

With my comment, the fact I was giving him attention although Rickey was tugging me away eagerly, Jeremey peeled himself off the wall, his sea-green eyes filling with life like I was accustomed to. A gift of his gorgeous white smile was given to me and an extra bonus of a kiss blown in my direction. That last one I could have done without.

"Whatever you wish, my pumpkin spice princess! Make sure you sit on my lap and give me a little dance; I'll need some healing after my scolding from Lady Edric!" His hands were cupped around his mouth as he waved me off, or was trying to beckon me over to him.

"You're still an ass, Darington!" I half-heartedly said, placing my other hand behind my back to give him the middle finger.

"Oh snap! Such vulgar behavior, Ms. Hemmingway. I'll have to punish you for that later."

Chief gave me an icy glare that we all noticed, making me stop my taunting. Jeremey did the gesture of a finger going in a circle he made with his opposite hand, licked his lips and kicked his butt with his foot, making my gut get twisted in irritating knots. Mr. Stillman chuckled when Prince of the Pervs walked over to the spot where he was, and I heard him exclaim, "Ah, youth..."

I wasn't sure if it was youth, environment, or my own sanity deciding to take a trip to Pluto during this critical mission, but regardless, I was letting Jeremey Darington worm his way into my life. I didn't like it or the fact I was accepting it. Change has never been overly good to me.

* * *

"Go ahead and set the watermelon by the lemonade, sweetheart." Mom pointed to the spot she was referring, the lovely, juicy color of the water-melon that was making my mouth, well, water, matching the pink checkered tablecloth. The glass table looked refreshing with these light decor touches, the blue outdoor umbrella blending with the perfect skies. I was happy the apple blossom and dogwood trees were blooming with the start of spring, the breeze dancing with petals, their scent filling my soul with a glowing light.

"These will go great with your burgers, daddy." I commented as I scooped out some pebble ice to munch on before dinner. It was a habit of mine to crunch on ice. I'm surprised I haven't broken my teeth yet, but it's better than picking my fingers when I'm nervous like I used to.

Dad moaned, putting his historical magazine article down to give me a look. "I'll get there kiddo. The charcoal needs to heat up." He loosely pointed his thumb toward the grill that was below us on the ground.

"When will Darius get home from work?" I inquired to my father, his clear-blue eyes looking up at the clouds, his glasses making a wink of light reflect off his gaze.

"Your brother said 3:30, but the boy is late even to his dreams, so I'd say we'd be lucky to see him by 4:00." Dad then went back to reading his article after examining the embers of the grill, smoke barely surfacing from them.

Mom gave an exasperated sigh, but gave a motherly smile straight after, talking to the air before looking at me, "I guess it's just good your brother got a job finally."

I rolled my eyes, popping a carrot stick dipped in ranch in my mouth. Mom smacked my hand with a spoon, never thrilled that I munch before big meals. I hated to tell her that wasn't going to change ever. "At least he finally got off his lazy butt. He still won't give me a discount easily when I buy my games there. Brat . . ." Darius worked at our local video game shop, where I got my fix for the latest *Pokemon* games, *Kingdom Hearts* goodies, and Funko POP figures that were invading my duplex worse than tribbles.

"You two still playing *Pokemon*? No one is better than Squirtle with those sunglasses." My dad quipped in, recalling the glory days of when *Pokemon* was new to the states and we were young and he was forced to watch it with us. Those were the days.

"Can't argue with the fact gen one is incredible, dad. But if we are strolling down my 90's childhood, nothing beats morphin' time!" I did my flawless Kimberly morphing into the pink ranger poses, my mother shaking her head, talking about the greatness that was Scooby Doo.

"*Go, go Power Rangers,*" Dad sang and gave a fist in the air. "Jason was the best and got ripped off when Tommy magically showed up . . ."

"Better be careful, father; Darius will kick your butt if he hears you bad-mouth his beloved green and white ranger role model." I warned, raising my eyebrow.

"Oh, whatever floats your boat. Now, in the words of General MacArthur—"

"You shall return." I finished his overdone history quote once he stood and went down the stairs. He gave me the Fonzie cool cat point and click before checking the grill.

A light gust picked up, the crackling of the tablecloth comforting as I stared off in the distance, seeing our fenced in yard where my parents' three dogs that I grew up with ran after balls, their tails wagging in time with the rustling of the leaves in our branches. A comforting contentment filled my soul, my hair whipping around me, around my thoughts. After all of the drama with the conflict between Jeremey and Rickey, I needed this planned weekend with my parents more than ever.

I never thought we were going to get out of Chief's verbal death grip. She even locked the door! The room was steamy, making you feel like there was a lack of oxygen. And Jeremey looked like he was beaten with a bat, after Chief gave him a, funny to me, giant goose egg on his noggin. Boy, he left our meeting with his tail between his legs.

A gentle hand was on my lower back, waking me up from my trip down memory lane. I turned with a small smile, easing into this transition of talking to mother, "How is school going?"

I leaned my elbow on the railing of the massive wrap-around, wood finished porch that my dad had always dreamt of having. When speaking of my little stars, a natural smile came on my face. I was very lucky getting to have my O.N.J. in the degree I went to school for. "Testing season is going to start soon, so things will be hectic for a month and then we have three weeks of trying to squeeze in learning when all they want to think of is our sports day, carnival, parents day, and our final book fair. I'm ready for that one! I think implementing the new sunshine summer readers program will help boost our sales and reading."

Mom nodded understandingly. We talked at least twice a week and kept each other informed on what was going on, same with dad, Darius, and grandma. My family means the world to me and has been there for me through true bad times, never judging me and only supporting me. They raised me to be cautious with the world around me, but to be me and show all how I shine as long as I work hard. I'm a realist like my father and a dreamer like my momma. The balance shouldn't work, but it does. I'm not 100% sure where Darius and I got our extreme nerdy obsessions, but they keep us bonded, joyous, and partly sane.

"Getting used to your new computer operating system?" I asked mom, taking a sip of the tiny bit of melted water in my ice cup.

"Yuck!" Mom made a face and rolled her eyes, making me giggle. "Stupid and our instructor is a real pill, a young guy who thinks he knows everything, but will run away when anyone asks him a question. Can't believe we have training for it for four years."

Dad walked up the stairs then, wiping his forehead before putting his beat-up Phoenix Suns hat back on his head. "She'll be a-cookin soon." After opening his magazine again, dad wrapped his arm around my shoulder and gave me a bump, an attention getter as he called it, on my head, giving mom a sophisticated look. "Teachers are always changing to meet the needs of the states for what's labeled as the newest, research-based program, but they change it after all that time learning it two or three years later. Just teach kids what they need to know. The modern world is making things so complex, eh Val?" A grin spread on my dad's face before he tussled my mom's hair. She swatted his hand away with ninja like precision. She must be where I got my reflexes for defending myself from. He tapped her back and then went into the house.

I popped a cherry tomato in my mouth, memories of picking these in my grandma's garden flooding into me, the ripe juices sending tingles of nostalgia inside me. A worried look entered my mom's deep blue eyes, one I have seen thousands of times, one that told me she was going into her full, loving mother mode. "And how is your . . . other job?"

Like most Hunters and Bringers, I was brought into the world of my organization and horrid *monstrum* through an incident that was out of my control. My parents had to watch me transition, see me scratched and harmed, confused and watch my life change before my eyes. Chief couldn't tell them about the existence of *monstrum* unless they saw them too, but they aren't dumb. My father is an American History professor and my mother a nurse in a geriatric psych unit, so they are very observant and astute in logic, all things medical, and me, their first child and only baby girl. Chief tried to convince them it was a weird animal attack, but they dismissed it, never fully buying it until I asked them to believe Chief.

Darius, being a nerd like myself, was quick to believe that this new world I was involved in was not natural, but perhaps supernatural. His first question for me after my incident was, "Is this from creatures that we see in our anime?" When I nodded, he understood, gave me a small hug, and swore he would protect mom and dad in their regular lives. Pretty mature for my baby brother who was lazy as a potato and had just graduated high school.

The solution now was a compromise. Families of those in The Hunters are protected. I felt badly that we had to move from the house we have lived in for fifteen years, but the organization found a wonderful home of the same size with every addition my father had always yearned for, his favorite being a small home gym and wrap around porch. They were slightly out of city limits, but still less than ten minutes from town in order to get groceries and for work. Close by is a house of Hunter guards that keep an eye on them in case my involvement with The Hunters would endanger them.

My family was aware that after The Hunters healed me, I decided to join them to help in their cause. Mother was scared I was being brainwashed by them, but that was not the case. It took me a while to convince them, but dad came around first and mom did follow. For their protection and per their contract with the government, all they know is I work for the government in addition to teaching, and going on assignments. But, I legally cannot disclose anything about my missions, job, co-workers, or travels. And, of course, no *monstrum* knowledge. They know my job is more than a secret agent, but for now, they are okay being in the dark and know not to ask. This is a pretty ironclad deal, but it will protect them. I wish I had more time to see them though.

I bit my lip, trying to process how I could avoid the topic of Jeremey at all, but mom saw my hesitation immediately. "I've noticed you've been distracted the past few weeks. They aren't working you too hard, are they now? Or making you do something dangerous?" Pure horror spread across my mother's face, her hands actually landing on her cheeks and mouth agape in parental concern. Her gears were spinning, her eyes darting every which way, imagining invisible to me situations of me getting eaten by the lion while walking the street.

I was a very loved and sheltered child, if that wasn't apparent.

"No, not much more than usual. Ms. Edric takes good care of me . . ." My parents had met Chief after the incident and had a special number to contact her with in case they had concerns. The first few months, mom called Chief all the time. It was sort of entertaining to see Chief's reaction when she saw my parents' number on her screen, and her informing me this was why she didn't have children in exasperated tones.

My pause made mom stare at me longingly, more panic growing in her expanding eyes. Better snuff out this fire before she locks me up in the guest room. But, the problem was, I wasn't sure I should even mention Jeremey or if so, how much. "We have sort of a delicate mission where I have to work with a new partner. It's just unusual for me to work with someone—"

"I thought Ms. Edric said you had a whole team working with you, so you're safe!" Alarm was seizing mom again. Time to bring her back.

"I still have a team that works with me overall, but in my department, it's usually me and I have to admit, I'm pretty good at what I do." I gave mom a teasing smile.

"A little confident, aren't we now?" She chided, poking my nose. "Do you and this new partner not get along?"

"Let me sneak on past you to get the ranch dip first." I popped a pretzel in my mouth, coating it in tangy white dip. Arg. Glad the Mayor of Perv City wasn't here, for he would have beamed and thrown out 'That's what she said.' Speaking of useless men. "The person I work with is okay, I guess. We're just very different. He can be very arrogant at times, full of himself—"

"*HIM?!*" Dad strode in, his brow creasing and face full of disapproval. "You don't need to worry about any guys, Val." Ah, the gruff voice telling me I'm not allowed to date. Haven't heard that in a decent amount of years.

"Now, now. Valda hasn't dated in a long time and she's a good judge of character. Besides, only one thing matters about him: How cute is he?" A sly grin was plastered on mom's face and her eyes sparkled with youth as dad scowled extremely hard, a bear like growl coming from his throat. I wasn't sure if I wanted to laugh or hurl myself off the rail at the thought of being with Jeremey. Ridiculous.

"Hm . . . I haven't really noticed . . ."

"Good, good answer. That's my good girl." Dad said in a breezy tone that was trying too hard, his nod final and determined.

"Sis is good at something? That's never happened before." The sound of my brother entered our ears as he hopped up the porch steps, swinging the keys to his green Ranger truck around his pointer finger. And yep, he had a Green Power Ranger bobblehead on his dashboard. Not as rad as my Ninja, but still pretty nerd epic, I had to admit.

"Ouch bro-bro. Look at you trying to be all intimidating in your game store smock." I leaned towards him, placing my hands on my hips to fully give him my sisterly sass.

He kindly replied by blowing in my face and flipping his shoulder length white-blond hair by my ear before going into the house.

"You two never stop pounding on each other, do you?" Dad grumbled, but was smiling with affection. He went to go check on how the hot dogs and burgers were coming. I liked mine black almost, but Darius didn't want any char on his. Such a noob.

"Yeah, that's never going to change daddy."

And as I soaked in the image of my father turning the delicious smelling meat on the grill and mom smacking my brother across the chest with a dish towel after he mentioned he was taller than her (only by two inches where I was five inches taller, so whatever), I once again felt a peace inside me, it rippling into all my cells to heal me. It was a challenge at times, being a Hunter, knowing I partly uprooted my family, making them worry, risking my life daily. But, I may not be here with them if I had been killed at the incident or on a mission. Eating watermelon with my parents, playing with my cuddly puppies, and discussing new animes with my brother was so simple, and so important to me.

Every small moment I can get with them is precious.

CHAPTER 10

"How'd you pick those thinly chopped onions out of there so easily? I've been picking them out since lunch started and I'm still getting baby chunks." Lindsey was bending over her plastic with pink polka dots lunch container while standing at the end of the hall, waiting for our students to be brought back to us from recess. Her hair was flopped on the side and distorted looking when I saw it through the container, like she had been in a food fight on only one side of her head.

"Chopsticks, my friend. They solve everything." It was the Monday after the weekend visit with my parents and brother and Sherri had made us a rocking meatloaf. However, she was aware both Lindsey and I loathed the texture of onions. She didn't give a rat's tail because she would always wag her sharp, ruby red painted finger and tell us how good they were for us. Her goal was to chop them up so finely that we'd never notice, but the force of our dislike for the veggie was strong. Momma Bear, deviously, also knew that we were too polite to pick them out in front of her. We all knew who was queen of this forest.

Christy bounced towards us with some lime green papers in her hand, her bottom nearly swishing with excitement like a cat waiting to show off a new toy. "I got 'em!" She held the papers up high above her head like they were the Holy Grail.

"Let's see them," I said encouragingly and she handed them over to me after waving them in the air like she was greeting the Queen of England. Lime green papers always meant teacher evaluations and both Christy, Lindsey, and I had them done every year for our first five years as a certified teacher, then it was every two after that. It was nerve wracking with two of my major weaknesses in life being a perfectionist and having an extreme fear of failure. Yeah, the lime green sheets were a death sentence it seemed for me. Damn lime paper!

I scanned carefully over the numbers while Lindsey struggled to get a pinch of meatloaf with no onion on it, for once not looking overly ladylike despite her cotton candy summer dress. Christy had gotten all 4's, which was excellent for our five point scale. I only noticed two 3.8s, but still, she did amazing.

"This is awesome! I'm so proud of you girl! Glad your work went noticed." I embraced her tight, feeling her large smile on my cheek. She has been working so hard for her kids since she became a young mom and always had a positive outlook. I'm glad some bonehead noticed.

Oh yeah. Mr. Devlin did.

"I'm sort of surprised they made Mr. Devlin do evaluations for non-tenure teachers. He's only been here a little less than a month. Oh kumquats!" Lindsey 'cursed' as she barely missed getting red sauce on her sugary-hued attire, her twisting her body at the last second for it to get on her snow white neck.

"Yeah, but he's doing such a great job considering. He's very person-able, upbeat, and has tried hard to get to know all the staff and their quirks. And it's good to see another man here, so our little guys can have a good male role model." Christy showed off another thousand watt smile.

"Yeah, too bad there isn't any here." I whispered to myself.

"Oh! Girls! In five days, it'll be exactly one month since Mr. Devlin has been here. I was thinking of making him cupcakes. I know they won't be as good as Ms. Candyfloss's, but I think that would be a good surprise! What color icing should I make?" Lindsey squealed all this as she wiped the sauce from her flesh, her grin near as bright as Christy's. I stepped back a bit, scared of getting sunburnt and I forgot my lotion.

"Oh! I love that idea. He does wear a lot of fun colored vests and ties. Maybe green? And he has a good sense of humor and works mostly with women, so pink would be fun too?" Christy chimed in.

"Those are both great ideas! I could use more than one color so people can pick or we could add rainbow sprinkles. Valerie, what color do you think he'd like?" Lindsey puppy cocked her head to ask me. I think she needs to get out of Lollipop and Rainbow Land.

"He'd probably say white." I volunteered, looking away from them for just a moment so they wouldn't see the evil tilt of my lips. Gosh, I know; I'm the worst.

Lindsey placed her perfectly manicured finger under her chin, staring up at the ceiling to roll my idea in her head seriously. "Hm . . . maybe. It sounds sort of boring to me. Ah! Unless you know he likes vanilla? Is that it?"

"No, but he deserves chocolate." I breathed out, my shoulders slumping, partly relieved and disappointed they didn't get my tacky jab at our boss.

"Because chocolate tends to be our school's favorite?" Christy asked to no one in particular.

"No, because he's a piece of crap . . ." I mumbled again, but the hens were too busy happily chuckling about sweets to hear me. Oh well.

"Valerie, did you get your evaluation done?" Christy inquired.

"No. I'll be the last one since it's only my second year. They did three in fall and I'll get my last one at the very end of the year. Honestly, the state isn't picky when I get them as long as I have four observations done to contribute to my evaluation by the end of May."

"You're really organized, girlie. I know Mr. Delvin will give you an outstanding score." Lindsey sighed, defeat all over her face, closing the lid to her yummy, but barely touched meatloaf. Curse onions getting in our way of nourishment!

I wasn't so sure about that. He said he really had a degree in administration, but our O.N.J. backstories were pretty detailed and our team knew how to fill in holes and train us to do so. He just seemed too irresponsible and goofy to be an administrator. He was more fit to play, well, Goofy at DisneyLand. He was a horndog too, so it worked.

The sounds of little feet that chorused into a stampede soon rang in our ears, the sound of this summoning us to once again become loving, nurturing teachers. The two and half hours left after school flashed by and by 3:15, after pick-up duty, everyone was in a rush to get home. Only Lindsey had five kiddos in afterschool tutoring, so the halls were clear when I took my long, but leisurely walk back to my classroom.

Strolling down the main hall with all the offices and storage rooms, way off in the distance, was our so beloved principal, walking towards my direction. However, he seemed dazed, his body so wound up that I could even see the tension through his immaculate deep chocolate brown dress shirt. Although he looked as well-groomed as the new norm, there was a haggardness to him, like he had just come back from war and barely missed the shockwaves of a deadly explosion. Even his hands were straight, swinging at his sides robotically.

I hadn't realized I had slowed my pace to a turtle crawl to observe him, the light from our wall-to-wall windows on my left side washing out the color of him. It was stunning that he hadn't noticed me yet, even though we were still a good fifteen feet apart. The middle door on my right, which was a restroom, creaked open and I leapt, unprepared for it. Coming out, unaffected by my yelp was Jimmy, an energetic young man in Lindsey's class who was staying for tutoring.

The boy skipped down the hall, unfazed about being alone as he headed towards Jeremey. When he recognized who he was, he bounded towards the principal and jumped up, beaming up at him with such joy that his red shirt seemed to stand out more. "Hi Mr. Devlin!" Jimmy exclaimed enthusiastically, like meeting his idol. At this age level, it was common for children to adore those in power, eager to please them and get their attention. And I knew that was what was happening here.

Mr. Fazed Today blinked slowly a few times before glancing down. His expression seemed like it was taking a while for him to register that a child was talking to him. Once he focused on the smiling Jimmy, a look of pure panic grabbed him, his eyes wide in shock and fear. But, after three short counts, he blinked rapidly, looking polite and very kindergarten principal, his tone to Jimmy warm and welcoming, "Hello there, young fellow. Are you off to go back to tutoring? Ms. Coleman will be missing you."

"I know! I had to use the bathroom, but she trusts me enough that I can go on my own." Jimmy danced on his toes like he had won a Little League Championship.

"Good for you! You keep up the all-star work there, my good man." He then gave Jimmy a slightly timid fistbump, his other hand twitching around his pants, vining into a quivering fist.

The little guy waved happily off and skipped around the corner to Lindsey's classroom, not noticing anything odd. I stood there, staring at a listless Jeremey, examining every angle of him for clues. When my vision went to his feet, I noticed dry mud around the edges of his usually crisp, designer shoes. The rustling of his hand being moved to rake through his spiky hair alerted me and we both looked forward, our eyes meeting.

When he realized it was me, his eyes had a glint winking in them and he strode up to me with a confidence that I was familiar with, but one I also wasn't. The closer he got, I picked up on the smell of his usual sandalwood cologne, but it was potent, enough to near make my eyes sting with moisture. Yet, mixed into that aroma concoction, I could smell the earth: mud, pine, musk, the wind adding fragrance to the fibers of his clothes, and the woods. It wasn't a bad scent, but it was too natural smelling for something in a manmade building, for someone I knew did run early each morning, but never carried more than a slight whiff with him. He was always careful with how he presented himself to others in every outing type, loving his expensive duds.

My first thought was that he had gotten more disturbing news on our *lamia* mission and we had to leave, but my gut was screaming inside me.

"Hello Val." His greeting was charming and full of poise as ever, but there was also a little bass and hardness in it I hadn't heard before, like he was rumbling a little in the back of his throat. Waves of sea-green examined me up and down thoroughly, a leer tugging at his lips.

"Good afternoon Mr. Devlin..." I hated how mousey my voice was coming out. My arms covered myself on their own, fearful of him trying to see through me. "You been running in the woods? Your military shiny shoes are caked in mud." I teasingly pointed out, a nervous smile forming.

He looked down and for a hair, he gave me a sly, slightly shy grin that made him look like an overly tired version of himself. "Yeah. I did some extra running over the weekend and tracked mud everywhere. It was nice to get out this morning too for an extra jog."

The statement seemed off to me, how you could get so muddy that it spreads to your dress shoes, but I brushed it off. In a hushed tone, I leaned my torso so I could keep this conversation between us, but my feet were planted in their spot in case I needed to flee, "Is everything okay with our assignment?"

Jeremey looked around over his shoulders and behind me, to see if anyone was around. When his sight landed on me once more, I saw a glimmer of deep brown surrounding his light irises again, like I did Friday evening with the conflict/dance battle with Rickey. Along with this, a shimmer of amber gold swam through the coloring of his eyes. The afternoon light from the windows was near blinding and when I searched for the odd colors again, nothing appeared.

A gruff chuckle came out of Jeremey's mouth. "Tsk, tsk, my little robin. Always in a hurry." He briskly gilded towards me, reaching out to move my hair away from my neck, his touch rough and blistering.

Uncharacteristically, he slammed his other hand by my ear with a flourish and stepped towards me, every mannerism and expression he was throwing at me illuminating raw power. Sure, he messed with me the first day in his office, but this seemed like he wanted me to think he was in charge. I stepped back, placing my hands casually at my sides to have more free ranged movement to strike him if necessary.

"How happy I am to be seeing you at work every day now." As his words got more tender, but commanding, whispers stopping the flow of time across the room, there I saw it again: the swirls of amber and brown ringing in his pupils. There was so much there now that the gentle sea-glass green was sinking, fading, almost crying for help. It was mesmerizing and terrifying all at once.

With my second of gasping, lost in the spell of his eyes, he reached up to trace my cheek. I was touched with chapped hands, hands that had been running in the woods all day it seemed, the aroma radiating off him confirming that too. Jeremey wanted to be affectionate, to take his time, savor this closeness, but the demanding look in his expression made it seem like a lie. I didn't know which side of him, the Rebel Alliance or The Empire, he was on. I did know this wasn't the Jeremey Darington I have had to tolerate for years and I wasn't gonna let him near me any longer.

When his other hand reached for the back of my head, I smacked it away, a loud sound popping through the space when we made contact. "BACK OFF!" I shouted as he slumped backward a little, my eyes burning with fury.

But the glare given back at me with a near snarl to match stomped out my fire immediately with its heated and destructive intensity. He gurgled loudly at me.

Before I could realize what was happening, Jeremey slammed me into the wall at lightning speed, making me see stars. But soon, those beloved little twinkles faded and were replaced with the mincing and determined face of this new version of Jeremey, one with a strength that seemed unorthodox.

Okay! He was pissing me off. "I don't know what you're doing, but if the organization gets word of this, I'll—"

I was cut off when his lips landed on mine, pressing my head back on the brick. The feeling and taste of his lips were searing, part of my heart leaping, trying to process what was happening and a hint of me lavished in it. But, there was no tenderness, no giving, no love, just an animalistic need and desire for his mouth to claim me. Jeremey continued to kiss me, my lungs hurting as they tried to gasp any oxygen into me. He jabbed his tongue down my throat and bit down on my lip hard, a sharp pain and wet feeling emerging from it.

I hadn't been kissed in so long, my stomach dripping with betrayal and chaos. I pushed his shoulders, but he was not budging, continuing this twisted make-out session. I even chomped hard on his lip, but this jerk just roared with delight and thought this was an invite for him to do the same, hard enough I was scared I'd have a scar. A tiny piece of flesh dangled from my lip and a few drops of blood cascaded down.

What was he doing? I was surprised he wasn't worried about passers-by, cameras, or our O.N.J.s being on the line.

He paused his lip lock, staring down at me with lust and triumph. My stomach felt like glass was slicing it from the inside and it burned just to take a breath. Moisture stung my eyes, the sight of him gazing down at me harder to see, but one thing stood out.

His eyes. The kind sea-glass green was no more, replaced with liquid gold slithering around, deep brown churning, and newest to this demonic color scheme? Blood red flashing strobe light style behind his eyelids. A million questions entered my mind, a thousand *monstrum* legends zipping through my noggin, but nothing was sticking.

"Val . . ." His voice rumbled once more as his thumb made circles along my cheekbone, his other hand trailing down my neck and then to the top button of my blouse. "You really have no idea how beautiful you are to me, do you?"

It was like he had razor sharp claws. I don't know how he did it, but with one shift swipe, he ripped the top button and material under my blouse in a jagged line. Horrified, I prepared to kick him where the sun never shines, but his movements were graceful and quick, him beating me to the punch of this tango. Once more, he kissed me longingly and ravishingly.

His hand traveled, tracing my spine, sending shivers down it. I felt him smile on my lips during our latest kiss. This was what I apparently needed to get a shock treatment back to my rational, Hunters self. It was as if ice water was thrown all over my face and I was alert.

My *sensei* didn't train a weak little samurai, so I slapped him so hard across his left cheek, the sound echoed eerily through the entire hall. Jeremey stumbled backwards, cradling his jaw. With one hand, my fingers gripped tightly to temporarily glue the rip in my blouse before cautiously creeping over to him, my other hand ready to break his skull with the next slap.

Shuffling up to his feet unsteadily, using the wall for support, Jeremey's hand shielded his eyes as if he had a massive headache. When he peered at me, the look in his eyes was one that could murder. The bloodlust in his irises, the red that could pass for blood dancing rapidly in his pupils, appeared ready to charge at me, but he didn't budge from his spot.

Because suddenly, a light went on in him.

Groaning, he rolled his head to the side a little and then raised it up to stare right at me, a look of pure shock all over his now ghost white face. His lips were quaking and hands trembling, but I ignored these for the moment. The first thing I wanted to check was his eyes. As he gawked at me, tracing his hands to see if they were really his, I was greeted back with the pretty sea-glass green pupils I was accustomed to. There was no amber, brown, or sinister red in sight, all those colors washed away from the shores.

Whatever I had encountered, whatever had stunned me, had not been Jeremey.

Pressing the cheek that had a good handprint mark etched into it, he finally spoke, his voice shaking, "Val . . . I don't . . . I don't understand how we're here. Why did you smack—" The question he was going to ask was lost in an eternal fog as he noticed the rip at the top of my blouse. My answer to his vanished question was a glare that became steely, frigid, and uncaring.

"Val!" Jeremey's voice was pleading now, desperate when he reached out towards me, but dared to not touch me. His eyes appeared to be holding back tears from the gleam in them. "Val! Oh my God . . . No. I . . . I didn't . . . I didn't do that . . . did I? Oh God! Val, I . . . I just . . . oh my God . . ."

A choking sob caught in his throat as he covered his mouth, his eyes still the size of saucers. He wasn't really denying kissing me, but it was like my slap had forced him to restart to his original setting

What scared me was I don't know now which one is the true Jeremey.

In a heated whisper full of hate, I told him how I felt, "Stay the hell away from me. I don't want you near me ever again." My eyes began to sting when I said this, refusing to look at him and his jackass face.

"Val . . ." I barely heard him utter, but the childlike anguish in it was pulling at my chest, the distress he was in impossible to not hear. In the corner of my eye, I saw him reach out to me again, but I ignored him.

"BASTARD!" I screeched, the windows shaking from the vibrations of my voice. Not caring if anyone heard, I bolted out the door in a dead run, sprinting down the hall, only looking at my feet and the shadows consuming me as I sped through the building.

I didn't care if someone saw me. Call the police. Get him fired. Serves him right. I didn't give a fuck anymore. Whatever that thing was, it was vile, unforgiving, and lustful. To think I was starting to at least accept Darington in my life and allow him to sink into my thoughts outside of our missions. Sometimes even, sickeningly, my chest thumped against my ribcage when I did.

It was like he was possessed . . .

Oh my fucking Lord.

Possession.

I nearly dropped my purse when I made it back to my classroom to swiftly grab it, this realization falling from the skies to bonk me. Could it . . . could it really be possible . . . ?

I shouldered my bag and darted out of the room, not wanting him to catch up with me. Regardless, I knew my next step: I had to report this to The Hunters.

CHAPTER 11

"Valda, sweetheart, are you sure you're alright?" Amy's memorizing brown eyes were brimming with worry, her mouth set in a deep frown. Absentmindedly, she stirred the Irish coffee in her antique white and blue patterned teacup she adored, the clicking sounding similar to guns going off in my pounding head.

I leaned back in my chair at the Hunter's Hub, blankly staring at an empty space on the pristine white wall, hoping it would blind me with its brightness. Or at least wipe my memory clean of what I just ran away from. "I . . . I don't know. My stomach is in knots after what happened and it feels like my brain is trying to download every thought since the dawn of time, but I don't have enough storage." I held my head at the last part of my explanation, waves of pain surging through my cranium, pulsing loudly in my ears.

About twenty minutes ago, after breaking several speed limits to get to the Headquarters in record time on my Ninja, I pried open the lab doors, maddeningly searching for someone to comfort me before I caved into myself. I staggered through the long halls, not registering any sounds or seeing anything clearly, my vision nearly covered in a film through all the tears I locked inside. Wandering, I let my tired feet be my guide, not questioning when I led myself to Amy's door. Silently, I turned the knob and let myself in, startling her at her desk a smidgen when I appeared in the doorway. Then, she soaked my image in.

I must have looked like a drowned dog because she ran to embrace me, a slew of questions flying my way, but I didn't hear many of her words. I was in a tunnel underwater and just trying not to lose my mind, everything distorting no matter if my eyes were opened or closed. I was Alice trapped within herself, my Wonderland fusing with my reality.

In a dragging walk, we ended up in the cafe area of the hub, after she brushed the soundless tears leaking out of me, then making sure no one was nearby. She ordered for us and then allowed me to sit and stare at my lap for a long time. Amy only rubbed my shoulder with sisterly affection, cooing me when I randomly leapt in fear out of my stool, recalling a random image of what happened.

Over time, I took a shaky breath and told her a waterdown version of what happened with Jeremey with many breaks in between to calm myself. Amy was very reassuring the whole time, her training and friendship to me shining every moment. I left out the extreme red flashes behind his eyes and my suspicions about him being possessed. In my tale, Jeremey kissed me roughly before I was able to escape after slapping his face. I did mention his strange behavior and the movement of gold in his irises the last two times I had seen him. I also asked Amy not to inform Chief yet. I was aware that I legally had to report this, but I wanted a bid my time to try to process a theory on why he would do this.

"Why are you protecting him?"

This was the first time she really spoke to me in fifteen minutes.

A surge of electricity ran up my spine, realization hitting me. I . . . I was protecting him. The dick forced a kiss with me and was making my head and insides a jumbled mess. I couldn't forget what he did, a video reel too vivid to destroy. Nor could I forgive him. There was no excuse for his behavior. Why was I not running to Chief to get him away from me?

Because a lost, but sure part of me knew that wasn't Jeremey, not really Jeremey.

GAH! My brain was a scrambled mush of colors and confusion.

My body, my essence, my mind, my gut, and my heart were all ripped in two, fighting with what I knew I should do and what I thought I knew about Jeremey. Those eyes . . . I have known Jeremey Darington against my will for three years now, encountering and bickering with him enough before we had this joint *lamia* assignment to know he has always had a breezy attitude and brilliant, unforgettable sea-glass toned eyes. I knew he had a past like we all did, that the sickest people could be the most charming on the outside. I wasn't stupid. I wasn't in denial. I was still livid, pissed beyond measure, ready to claw his flesh myself for what he did.

But, I was torn. And the battle raging hot inside me made every part of me shut down.

Slowly, my head feeling it weighed a ton, I fearing I could not support myself. I attempted to answer her question. My voice was soft and wispy, "I don't know, Amy. I'm not a weak person, you know that. I have this very powerful drive to test the sharpness of my *katana* on him for what he did, right down the middle to practice symmetry. But, something strong is pounding in the cracks in my armor, whispering to me that the man who did kiss me so roughly wasn't Jeremey, not the one we know. It sounds crazy and I don't want to defend him, but . . . OH! My body's a mess right now!"

I grabbed my hair and rocked in my stool, my fear of being unbalanced keeping me steady. The roots of my hair protested, informing me I was gripping my head too hard. I have never felt so out of control of myself due to a person and I just wanted to sink into myself.

"You're not crazy for thinking that way, Valda. As a fellow woman, I'd say kick his ass into the atmosphere and let him land on his chin in Timbuktu." Even I had to chuckle at that. "And we will have to cross that bridge soon about informing Chief. But . . . you know more than I do that in our field dealing with the powers of *monstrums*; you can't rule anything out. You need to be extremely careful, Valda. Tell Ms. Edric every detail, and Mr. Stillman too, that way they know how to deal with the situation."

The pat of her hand sent warmth into my veins, but I still felt like a shell of myself. I made the choice to not open my heart for a long time, and the fact Jeremey decided when I was going to attempt to do this, even if he ends up being possessed, made every part of me feel rubbery and fake.

"Val? Do you . . . do you want me to Erase?" Amy asked with pure compassion, but a note of seriousness in her voice. Her eyes became doe-like and her skin losing some of its color.

I snapped in attention, the thought never dawning on me. The true maximum ability a *kotodama* had: memory sweeping. And with her skill set, my friend could easily make one select memory vanish or years blink away into a void. This power is why many fellow Hunters either call Amy a *monstrum* in human flesh or are fearful of her, her level of mastery in this task both artful and terrifying. I trusted Amy one-hundred percent, but I didn't want to be on the end of her ultimate reason for her being on our team.

"No thank you," I said humbly, watching the baby puffs of steam from my second cup of hot cocoa, grateful for it for distracting me.

A look of relief washed over her pretty face, Amy fanning herself to try to hide her discomfort. "I didn't think you would, and I'm glad. As you know, the feelings associated with any event I Erase stays, even though the memories are gone. I don't recommend it by choice."

I nodded, my ears then picking up the light tapping of wedges and the shuffling of papers. Before turning toward the sound, I knew right away who it was. Happy I was correct, in the distance, I saw Kesler and Bonnie walking side-by-side, both of them laughing with rosy cheeks at something. Kesler was carrying her research books and she was very thankful for it with the batting of her long lashes. The beams on their giggling faces and sparkle in their eyes as they walked towards the cubicle area in their own little world made me want to believe that everyone got that sort of charming life. By touching my lips though, I brought back all the ache of knowing my first kiss in years was not of my choosing.

Sighing, I stared at Amy, feeling I had aged fifty years. "I'm glad those two are getting along so well. I'd be nice if I can help everyone preserve those lives. It's gonna be hard to work with Darington, but as long as we can take down the *lamia*, that is what I'll focus on. I don't owe him a damn thing."

"You're right on that. You do what you need to do, but know you are worth so much more than you see. I'm here Valda, as your counselor and dear friend. I'll support you anyway I can." The clock in the hub chimed at 4:30, meaning I needed to get ready for my work-out session at the gym. My limbs felt like Jell-O and even my hair hurt, but I forced myself to stand. I shakily stood up with the support of the stool. Concern shone in Amy's eyes then, her tone gentle as she continued, "But, you need to tell Chief as soon as possible or I will have to."

I bobbed my head a fraction, understanding I didn't want to put her in that situation. "Yeah, I'll go workout to clear my head and face the music with Chief and Mr. Stillman. Thank you for being there for me. You're the best."

"It's what friends are for." She came over to me then and gave me a warm embrace before venturing off to her office.

It was a struggle to walk normally. As I waddled near to the far right exit, I stepped on something hard and lumpy. Startled, I moved my foot to see a little gold and rose pink gem-studded bear keychain was what I stepped on. I picked it up to examine it and saw a piece of sky blue lanyard tied on the keyring. That was the color we used for our ID badges . . .

No one was around, so I placed it in my pocket and journeyed onward to the gym, dragging myself around like I was useless weight with an over-crowded brain. I guess I was.

* * *

I felt like my feet had concrete blocks attached to them as I pushed myself to walk to the gym. Too tired to keep the jumbled words that pretended to be thoughts and the colors that were lying sights at bay. Wriggling the edges of the pink towel around my neck for dear life was only a baby salvation. The red of my old track shirt seared my eyes, my neck not having the energy to be held up. For the first time in ages, I didn't have the desire to work out, but I was praying the excretion of my muscles would help me tune out the sizzling pain I had stabbing my temple.

The sliding doors greeted me, welcoming me into the sacred space of the gym, shiny and sparkling from a recent cleaning and disinfecting. The treadmill seemed like a good place to warm up. I tried to listen to my music, but my melodies betrayed me today, giving me too much empty space to let my thoughts bury their way deeper into my mind and emotions. I sighed and jerked the earbuds out after trying three different songs.

Choosing the dull sounds of the T.V., my beloved *Munsters* on the screen, I allowed myself to space out. Nothing was sticking, but at least it was better than getting crushed by my own questions: Why did Jeremey do this? Why did I not kick his ass afterwards? Why did I not tell Chief yet? Why did I even care at all? Why was I getting confused, letting him get to me? Why? Why? WHY?! Too many dammed unsolvable mysterious and I hated being in the dark!

After only twelve minutes, I felt weak and feverish, like I was a sick person trying to run a marathon. Dizzily, I got off the treadmill, using it for a crutch, grateful no one else was in the gym. I usually only feel this puny when I get sick once a year. I guess my soul was ill. Limping over, I went to sit at the metal bench by the door, my breath coming out in ragged puffs. Sweat formed above my eyebrow. My stomach felt like I would vomit up acid.

I had to stop thinking about this. I was literally making myself sick. How weak I sounded! He's not worth any thoughts or time! I took a swig of ice water from my Power Rangers bottle, but it didn't fuel me with superhero motivation; it only made me sad, washed out, done. I wished I could travel to a land of my animes, even if I had to fight for my life. I could deal with *monstrums*, but I couldn't figure out how to deal with mortals with the hearts of one.

My head slumped down and I rested my elbow on my knee to hold my twitching eye. I was a broken doll, the light mocking me with its too harsh glare. The swishing of the automatic doors sounded like banshee calls hammering my damaged eardrums—

"Val . . . ?"

A timid murmur of my name being uttered felt like a slap, my eyes engulfing my face. Although I felt miserable, I snapped my head in attention to see the brut who caused this emotional damage mess I was. Jeremey was standing there in the semi-dark, staring at me with eyes of utter pain and affection, like I was a precious child who witnessed the world being destroyed in front of me. It took him great effort to stand normally, a hard act as his muscles looked frozen in place through his shirt and his hands were shaking from what looked like nerves.

Sea-green eyes, the hue of glass on a white sandy beach, greeted me at his entry. That was reassuring at least. But seeing his whole presence spiked my fear, my confusion, and my rage.

My voice sounded rough and foreign, as if I was speaking through a straw with water in it. "I told you to stay the hell away from me . . ." I glared at the floor so hard I thought I would burn a hole in it. I refused to meet his gaze unless I had to.

"Val . . . Please . . . I just . . . I need to apologize. What I did . . . it was totally wrong . . . and not who I am." I saw his shadow adjust on the floor as he continued to speak through what sounded like a sob in his throat, "I want you . . . to understand that. You're . . . you're someone I never want to hurt . . ."

I mechanically moved my head up to look up at him dead-on, my hands turning purple at the fingertips for me squeezing them for dear life, my anchor so I didn't sail away into nothingness like I yearned to. "Why . . . ?" It was barely a faint of a whisper I choked out, but it echoed across the room, the venom tone that naturally came out making Jeremey flinch.

Jeremey's face paled, as his feet fidgeted, debating if they wanted to move or not. With a hard, painful sounding sigh, he spoke after his head flopped down to study his shoes, "I . . . I can't tell you. I can't tell you why I did it. God, I wish . . . But . . . I'm . . . I'm sorry Val . . . I can't . . ."

I pried my hands apart, fusing them together on either side of me to make fists that trembled fiercely. I needed to get out of here. The hues around be were swirling, my chest aching, a weight being pressed against it. Everything he first explained to me seemed like what I stupidly wanted to hear: that none of this was his fault, that some other power was at work. But now, he couldn't trust me to tell me what happened. I didn't want to be his damned partner anyway, but now after this, when a sliver of a fraction wanted to believe he had a good heart deep down, he can't tell me, he can't trust *ME*?

Even though I thrive to be as tough as nails, I'm actually delicate, like glass. My older self was resurfacing, the one I tried to hide. And . . . I'm about to shatter.

Out of nowhere, Jeremey's pity party ceased and he animatedly shouted, pleading with every syllable, "Val! I can't apologize enough! I know this will change our relationship—"

I didn't want to hear him speak any longer, his voice a knife stabbing me. "Shut up . . ." I mumbled through clenched teeth, sweating dripping down my face.

He didn't hear me and went on, "I won't let this affect our mission. We swore to protect others. And I will do that, including protecting you—"

"Shut . . . up . . ." I dragged out in a heartless hiss, spit bubbling in my mouth.

I felt drugged, lines of tint blurring my vision. My veins became icy, goosebumps pricking my skin. I could feel my heartbeat thudding, hammering, in my ears. Sounds zoomed in and out at different frequencies like I was in a tunnel with echoing surround sound speakers playing every song known to man at once. Nothing made sense. Everything twisted inside me, all the emotions I was capable of knotting into one and my body couldn't handle it. I was going to explode.

He went on, "I just want you—"

"Shut up . . ."

"To—"

"SHUT UP!" I shrilled, the crack in me too great, destroying the whole frame I was. The feelings in my body erupted out of me in a scream of pure rage that made an impact. The ceiling to floor mirror that was set into the wall behind me shattered, shards raining down on both of us, littering the floor with pings that rippled our personal sound barrier.

Jeremey's eyes engulfed his face, the sea-color of them foaming a pinch with horror-stricken white. His body became rigid as he stepped back a pace. Confusion was radiating off him. The world was painted in a red-tint to me, my eyes burning with merciless drive, my sole wish for Jeremey to vanish out of sight. The shards of glass were jagged, some blade-worthy sharp as they poked my skin on their descent. The cuts did not affect me, blood only fueling the fire in my soul. Seconds seemed to turn into minutes, my vision no longer clouded, but able to clearly see each freeze-frame of the mirror's breaking.

The reflective rain I caused, many the size of pebble ice, cascaded down when I barely moved my head and when they fell in front of me, I saw an image of myself, the way I must have looked to Jeremey.

I didn't like what I saw at all.

My blind-sided fury changed into shock, my knotted up emotions once again coiling up inside me, terrified of coming out into the light again. My body was okay with the pain I was in as long as I didn't break another time. My mind was hollering at me, interrogating me about what I had done, why I could have done it, how I could have. My spirit was telling me I had to be stronger than this, that even though I was hurt and disoriented by the kisses Jeremey gave me by force, I had to stop . . .

Shoes clicked softly together, this tap of a noise bolting me to re-notice Jeremey in the room. His feet were together again, no longer trying to flee, but his expression was one of pity, uncertainty, and timid, tender affection, the green in his eyes floating on clouds, slightly hazy. He studied me, squeezing his hands into fists pinned at his sides.

"Val . . . ?" He barely managed to squeak out of his agape mouth.

Our eyes met as I tried to understand what had happened, but I didn't have the time, our concerns placed on hold when Kesler barged into the room with a cherry red face, breathing cartoonish and weak.

"Ms. Hemmingway! Emergency! Chief needs . . . AH!" Kesler screamed, cutting off his notification when he saw the glass all on me and on the floor. The poor dear's face became paper white and clammy. I thought he might have fainted with how he swayed.

"Ms . . . Ms . . . Ms. Hemmingway! Wha . . . What . . . What in the world . . . happened?!" Kesler yelled, upset at the whole ordeal.

I stood in silence for more counts than I should have, staring ashamed and blankly at my young friend, not sure how to explain myself. My words were locked tight.

Surprisingly, Jeremey stepped between the two of us and spoke on my behalf, "It's sort of my fault, Kesler. Agent Hemmingway and I had a disagreement again, and she got upset at a sexist, piggish comment I didn't really mean, hitting the mirror with her fist. We had no idea the mirror would shatter. Either Agent Hemmingway is up there with Bruce Lee as a martial arts legends or this state-of-the-art facility is faulty." He gave Kesler a coy little smile and arched his eyebrow, trying to smooth his honest sounding and compassionate explanation with some humor.

Why was he defending me? True, I didn't want anyone to think I was a freak and I wasn't in a state to vouch for myself, but after everything that's happened . . . I was confused more than ever.

Mentally, I put a lid on my messed up life and viciously brushed the glass shards out of my hair so I didn't look so hellishly ragged. I'm sure I had a lion's mane, but I didn't care. I huffed out some tightness that was wound up in my gut to get the courage to look at Kesler, sitting again. I had a mission to do after all. "What sort of emergency, Kesler?"

My friend played with his fingers in mid-air, looking every which way, a composing method he did when stressed. "It's, ah . . . well . . ."

"Hey, kid! What is taking so damn long? I got the W.A.V. all prepped. She's a' itching for some action and you're delaying her. Is the pansy Bringer boy stalling us?" A large hand clamped down hard on Kesler's tiny shoulder. He squealed like a frightened baby pig when Galen did this, the big weapons specialist looking like the head of a crime gang in his all black outfit and trench coat. Galen's manly pout was impatient, but his eyes were beaming with the thought of adventure, even his scar looked pulsing with delight.

Jeremey and I exchanged a glance and a mutual agreement silently sang between us. There was intense tension we would have to deal with and work around, but for now, we pushed it aside. The air was thick with it, but our vows as a Hunter and a Bringer rang truer and from the stances of my two cohorts, this was serious.

"What's going on?" I asked, still staying in my bench seat, but focused on Galen.

He cocked his head a bit, seeing the broken glass for the first time. The question flashed in his eyes, but only for a second before he gruffly explained, "Chief is sending the four of us out now for a mission. Your O.N.J. has already been called because we're not sure how long we'll be gone. The Bringers' fancy helicopter is waiting for us outside and my W.A.V. will be tailing us in one of our Hunter's military planes. Chief already has the intercontinental emergency backpack on board Spike's here Charger hunk-of-metal too." He jabbed his thumb hard out into the hallway, his face neutral.

"A new development in our case?" Jeremey inquired inquisitively.

Galen shoved Kesler forward, him having to windmill his arms funnily in order to keep is balance, a goofy sound coming out of his mouth. Once he got back into a standing position, he cleared his throat and told us a tale that made the room lose suction. We became so silent that you could hear a pin drop:

"A slaughter has occurred in Europe and from the descriptions of witnesses who saw the murders and the kidnapped victims leave blankly from the scene . . . it sounds like the *lamia* in your case, and he had another with him, a being with a strange voice and swirling red eyes. They were in the boot of Italy. Now, it seems, they are heading in the direction of the coast of Greece . . ."

To be continued in:

The Hunter and The Bringer Book 2:

MONSTERS
AND MORTALS

BONUS FEATURE:
THE HUNTER AND BRINGER
Q&A SESSION

Four years ago, my amazing publisher and neek friend, Sheenah, gave me a fun, unique challenge: I was asked questions for my blog, a fairly normal sounding procedure, but my characters 'came in' and answered the questions for me in all their, ah, 'charm.' This was for my main series, *Spirit Vision*, Stary and Umbra stealing the stage.

Recalling this fun tidbit, I thought it would be fun to bring this back as a bonus feature for my readers to thank them for their patience with me and eagerness for my new book. This time though, it's for the two main characters of this book, *The Hunter and The Bringer*.

Without further ado, enjoy this interview of Valda Hemmingway and Jeremey Darington!

* * *

Introduction by Valda Hemmingway: Hello everyone! My name is Valda Hemmingway, but I go by Val to my family. My boss informed me I needed to do this interview for our beloved patron, Mrs. Morgan Straughan Comnick. She apparently got permission from the government to write a book about my strangest and toughest case to date, so, if you're reading this, that means you know about my 'real' job and are sworn to not tell a soul, unless you want your head sliced off by my katana—

(Voice from behind): Now, now, my sexy lady; we don't want to scare off these charming people, especially the delicate ladies . . .

Val *(Turns, surprised, then annoyed)*: Darington? What the flying flips are you doing here?"

Jeremey: This is our mission, so I'm apart of the interview for Mrs. Comnick, and might I add, she's such a fox. So whimsical bubbly, full of sunshine . . . and those long legs and hot ass . . .

Val: Lord! You are so disrespectful! I can't believe Chief sent you down here nor that Mr. Stillman has to see your face daily. Don't talk about Mrs. Morgan that way!

Jeremey: Don't worry now, my little flower; you're the only fox I want to pet . . . **Gives a sexy glance**

Val: GAH! Moving on! Let's just start this interview so I can get away from you faster!

Jeremey: Ouch! Feelings, dear! But we should begin for Mrs. Comnick's honor and the beautiful lady readers." **Leans towards the crowd seductively and unbuttons his collar button** Hi. I'm Jeremey Darington, and I dare you not to fall in love with me, but know my heart belongs to Val, during work at least . . .

Val *(Mouth agape, irritated horror on her face)*: I . . . I . . . I have no words. *Facepalm* Shall we start, please?

1) WHAT IS THE STORY OF THE NOVEL?
Val: *The Hunter and The Bringer* is about a joint case between two rivaling *monstrum* hunting organizations, The Hunters and The Bringers. Obviously, these two have extremely different views on how to handle the monstrum, but a *lamia*, or vampire as you mortals may refer to it, has powers beyond

what we have seen. Myself and Dofus over there are the best agents in our organizations and are forced to work together to track this *lamia* in order to save more innocents from being abducted or killed. It's not easy for us to work together by any means!

Jeremey: Awww, come on, cupcake! Although that was a lovely explanation of the general plot of the incredible Mrs. Comnick's work, it seems you were favoring one of the organizations over the other. I thought we were a team!

Val: Well, yeah! I am part of the Hunters. It makes sense for me to favor one side. I figured you were getting all bent out of shape because I called you a Dofus.

Jeremey: Oh, no, little butterfly. I know you call me names because you are a sweet little, lethal girl that has a playground crush on me. I bet you look adorable in pigtails." *Places hands on face and squeals with delight*

Val: . . . I'm gonna punch you in the throat and taser your ass.

Jeremey: Oooh! I like them spicy!

2) CAN YOU PLEASE TELL US ABOUT YOURSELVES?

Jeremey: Oh! I'll start! Hello ladies. My name is Jeremey Darington. I'm 33 years with sea-glass green eyes and a spiky, perfect mesh of dirty blond hair, and yes, I work out. I enjoy designer suits, shoes, and watches, pop songs, all sports, but I like football the best, going to the gym, being a principal, meeting new people, bur smoking hot ladies are my favorite. I just want to meet someone special, someone I can hold hands with, where we can gaze longingly into the sunset on a sandy white beach . . .

Val: You sound like a dating site ad. *Rolls eyes* Konnichiwa minna-san. I'm Valda, Val, Hemmingway. Kindergarten teacher, top-notch agent for The Hunters, and all around nerd. My favorite hobby is anything to do with Japanese culture: history, language, sword techniques, cosplay, manga, anime, and traditions. I also love combat training, 80s to early 00s cartoons, fashion, toys, and music, walking, singing, acting, history, doing fun projects with my students, Dungeons and Dragons, *Pokemon*, and collecting necklaces, stuffed animals, and Elvis merchandise. That's probably more than enough about me. Sorry about that.

Jeremey *Jotting notes in a notepad*: I hope I roll a 20 when I get alone with you, my elf princess.

3) CAN YOU HELP ME DEFEAT MY ARCH NEMESIS: GERTRUDE VON GUMBYWAPPER?

Val (*Intense look to the camera and in a frantic, fast voice*): What sort of *monstrum* is this Gumbywapper? How have they hurt mortals? Number of incidents? Level of *monstrum*? Describe their attacks? Do you know their country of origins?

Jeremey: I take cash, checks, and German chocolate as payment. As long as this Gummywapper doesn't stain my silk shirts, I'm game.

4) IF YOU HAD A SUPERPOWER (THAT YOU DON'T ALREADY), WHAT WOULD IT BE?

Val: Psychic abilities like Professor X and Jean Gray, prior to the Phoenix arc. Flying, force shields, helping others who are falling, and reading minds. It'd be pretty baller. Although, Shadowcat is my favorite X-men.

Jeremey: I don't need superpower; I'm already too perfect and any more would be overkill. *Winks*

Val: Maybe I could projectile you off the building right now . . . or make your mind explode like *Star Trek*.

5) WHAT INSPIRED YOUR BOOK COVER?

Val: The insanely talented Ms. Suzy Zhang made the cover for our book. She also makes the covers and bookmarks for Mrs. Comnick's young adult series, *Spirit Vision*. Ms. Zhang did an incredible job! It could not be any more perfect."

Jeremey: I give it a 9.5 out of 10 stars. *Crossing arms with a smug smile*

Val: Really?! What could possibly be wrong with it?!

Jeremey: Oh no! Nothing is wrong with it. Ms. Zhang did a beautiful job on the covers, but it's impossible to capture my studiness unless they study me up close. And I hope that will be your job, Val. Wanna play doctor?

Val: You'll need one if you insult Ms. Zhang's work again.

6) WHAT GENRE WOULD YOU SAY THE BOOK IS?

Val: *The Hunter and The Bringer* would be in the supernatural category, but Mrs. Comnick likes to add sub-genres: humor, slice of life, acceptance, nerd culture, mystery, and more."

7) WHAT IS THE TARGET AUDIENCE?

Jeremey: This book is new age/older young adult, so 17+.

8) WHAT KIND OF RESEARCH DO YOU DO WHEN WRITING?

Val: At our headquarters, we have to study about every "mythological" *monstrum*: their history, origins, attacks, physical characteristics, diet, and more. We are placed in simulations to help us train to encounter as many monstrums as we can prepare for. We are also trained in an assortment of weapons, self-defense, chemical compounds, and martial arts in order to defend ourselves and defeat them. So we research all the time. And that doesn't even include all the individual cases we have to do custom research for. That's why I'm glad we have such an all-star team to make this come together.

9) HOW DO YOU SELECT THE NAMES OF YOUR CHARACTERS?

Val: My name means the power to rule. I think she just liked the last name Hemmingway and it seems to fit me well.

Jeremey: My name is a unique spelling of Jeremey. Mrs. Comnick likes to add little twists to her characters' names at times. It means exalted; I so see that. Darington is sort of a play on words with how bold and daring I am, in my profession and with my lady love here. My name and look is actually loosely based on one of Mrs. Comnick's first bosses in education.

Val: Poor Mrs. Comnick, having to deal with a real-life you.

Jeremey: You mean lucky!

10) WHAT IS THE MOST DIFFICULT PART OF YOUR WRITING PROCESS?

Val: Mrs. Comnick wrote in her notes that the hardest things for her is time management now that she works so hard at other jobs. She wants to make the books the best they can be, for her readers and for us. We're very grateful for that.

Jeremey: Our fantastic author also says that marketing is a challenge since she didn't get a business degree!

11) DO YOU HAVE ANY PETS?

Val: I have a beautiful kitty named Socks, who is the love of my life! My dad found her as a stray with her momma when she was only 5 months old, but her momma's a free spirit and stays outside near my parents' house. My baby girl has gray fur with some dark stripes, green eyes that flash gold when she's hyper, two perfect bullseyes, one on each side, the cutest cheeks and two-toned nose, and little white feet, hence her name. I just love her to pieces! *Happy squeal*

Jeremey (*Mumbles and looks down at the floor in annoyance*): Hmph! I thought I was the love of your life ... Anyway, I really don't like animals that much, so I don't have any.

Val: You should be caged up. My parents' precious dogs are way better than you.

Jeremey: Well, I am too much of an animal to be contained. Woof, Woof!" *Licks lips*

12) DO YOU HAVE ANY SECRET TALENTS?

Val: Well, I can make my lips go over my nose and am fairly double jointed in my arms and elbows. It comes in handy or can be a cool party trick.

Jeremey: I can get every eye to look at me when I enter a room.

Val: Cocky son of a bitch . . .

13) OPPOSITE END: DO YOU HAVE ANY QUIRKS YOU WISH YOU COULD STOP?

Val: When I get nervous, I tend to run my fingers through my hair or on occasion, I pick at my fingers. I wish I could stop that.

Jeremey: I pop my toes when I'm bored, hence why I wear tighter tip shoes, so it's harder to do it in.

Val: That's disgusting and not healthy.

Jeremey: Awwww! You care about me, poppet? Give me a hug. *Runs towards Val with arms opened*

Val *Punches Jeremey in his chest* **:** Stay away from me or there will be a katana between us next time.

14) WHAT IS YOUR FAVORITE FOOD?

Val: Cheese! I'm even in a Cheese-aloic group.

Jeremey: Meat, and I know you'll want some, baby.

Val: None of yours.

Jeremey: Ouch! Shot down!

15) WHAT PHYSICAL FEATURE DO YOU WISH YOU COULD CHANGE ABOUT YOURSELF?

Val: A lot. I really don't think I'm that pretty.

Jeremey: Valda Hemmingway, truly, you are the most divine creature on the planet. You're perfect; never doubt that.

Val: . . . I, ah . . . well . . . Can we move on?

Jeremey: Valda, are you blushing?! Oh I think you are!

Val: Shut up, Darington!

Jeremey: I mean, the universe knows I am perfect in every way, especially with my dripping good looks . . .

Val: . . . You're such a pig . . . I . . . AH! *Goes in to chop Jeremey's neck*

Jeremey: Whoa! Babe, stop. We just . . . go so well together . . . AH! *Falls over, shielding self*

Mrs. Comnick: And I think we're done here! Thank you everyone for reading the Q and A session conducted by Val and Jeremey. I'm glad I got to share this experience with them . . ." *ducks from a flying chair with loud crashes and pleading coming from the background*

What chaos have I unleashed on the world?

Thank you to everyone who submitted questions for this feature! You guys rock!

Acknowledgements

Thank you to my lovely writer cohorts who believed in me every step of the way, knew my struggles and still gave me light, love, and criticism, even if I didn't like it:

My beautiful Beta Readers: the superb in every manner Dan W. and my gem and fellow fangirl, Julie. May all your dreams come true like you helped me with mine.

My fellow companions of words: Dan Coglan, Alesha, Danny B., Kate, and Casey, who fuel my creativity and drive.

My ravishing and talented formatter, Sheenah, for sticking with me, being the balance I need in my writing career, and my Disney sister.

My insanely talented artist, Suzy Zhang, for making my visions come to life, making me feel special and important, and is like a sister to me.

To my adoring family:

My mom, for being my precious friend, the one who understands me, comforts me, and tells me to be the shine in the world as myself.

My daddy, for being my supporter, my guide to life, and a treasure I know who will always remind me how dear I am.

My little brother Miles, my best friend, my goofball partner in crime, the one I truly can tell anything to. We always have each other's backs.

My big brother Jon, so hard working, understanding, and patient. I have always looked up to you and always will.

My grandma Shirley, for being my angel on Earth, my favorite person, my caretaker, my laughter, my light.

My in-laws and Comnick family: Bruce, Jolleen, Janet, Bob, Nathan, and everyone. for adopting me, letting feel their overflowing love and warmth, and showing their pride in me. They are like sunshine.

My family, the Hutchings and Straughans, for giving me my roots so I could reach towards the skies, blooming in your affections.

To my fur-babies Cookie and Gabby and those in Heaven: Lancey and Winnie. Thank you for all the love, cuddles, and being true friends I could always count on and be myself with.

To the man of my life, my love, my darling, my sun, moon, and stars. You are my healer, my embrace, my companion in every meaning, my gift I can never repay. You have seen me through all the good times and stressful ones and still see the great in me I rarely see in myself, but you help me learn. I love you with all that I am. And I would be lost without my precious kitty Socks; how she fills my heart with joy!

To my friends who have never left me even when darkness descends, who stand up for me, who help me travel the difficult at times path of life: Tabby, Nathan B., Andrew, Kristen, Micah, my Oneechan Sarah, Christy, Sherri, and others. I love you all.

To all my co-workers at FALC: Mr. Dunivan, Janis, Kim, Katie, Kurtis, Danny, Kristie, Karen, Donna, Billi, Pat, Missy, Paul, Mike, Todd, Tuck, Brenda, Jaime, Mr. White, Officer Musgrove, Officer Myer, and all my precious students. I am so grateful for how we are a family to every student that comes in through our doors and how we support each other. I care for my students deeply and am so lucky to be in such a loving environment.

I will always be a Knight in my heart, but I am honored, humbled, and proud to be a Blackcat! Thank you for hiring me.

To Mrs. Long for being so supportive in spreading my nerdy ways creatively, oddly, and bigly with my Anime Club students. Anime Club, you guys make every day an adventure and I enjoy our time immensely. I am proud to be your *sensei* and want to give you the fun, memories, and knowledge to spread your *otaku* wings.

To my church family and my Lord, both for keeping me strong in faith, always lending me a hand, being there for me no matter what, giving me a confidence boost when I fall, and for allowing me to be the teacher to our little ducklings, a job I treasure. I am so lucky my God led me to you all. And a major congratulations to my soon to be priest, Richard! You have worked so hard and deserve more than words can express!

To my beloved mentor, friend, and ray of sunshine that led me down my path to teaching and compassion, Ms. Mahan, my special teacher who gave me song and love, Mrs. Sue Bauche, my high school mother Mrs. Stroud, the man with the charm and energy that started my writing dream, Mr. Banger, and every teacher that has had to put up with me. Thank you for giving me the knowledge to succeed.

To my beloved Missouri, for being my muse, my home, and my safe haven.

To my fellow con and *otaku* pals. Let us rule the world with our childlike hearts, fun-loving souls, and never-ceasing wonder! I especially want to thank my con sister and superfan: Cat. You, my lady have helped me out so much this year and fangirling with you make my heart full and giddy.

For my doctors who have guided me this year with my transition with a life of lupus and to those who care enough to check on me: my family, my love, my friends, my church, my co-workers (especially Todd, Mr. Dunivan, Paul, and my giving mentor Janis), and my students. Some days are a struggle, but you guys make me want to fight it harder, and I will. To all who have lupus, I know your pain and support you in every way. You are not alone.

And to you, dear reader. None of this would be possible without you. You have made my dreams of writing in the stars come true six times now, and I hope these books give you a little light in your life. I love all of you!

Until we meet again in the pages of a book:

Love,
Morgan Straughan Comnick

About the Author

Educator of young minds by day, super nerdy savior of justice and cute things by night, Morgan Straughan Comnick has a love for turning the normal into something special without losing its essence. Morgan draws from real life experiences and her ongoing imagination to spark her writing. In her spare time, she enjoys doing goofy voices, traveling to new worlds by turning pages, humming child-like songs, and forcing people to smile with her "bubbliness." It is Morgan's mission in life to spread the amazement of otaku/Japanese culture to the world and to stop bullying; she knows everyone shines brightly.

For more information about Morgan, the *Spirit Vision* series, and her other works, check out her website, which also have links to all her social medias: http://morganscomnick.com